By the same author

PLANS FOR DEPARTURE

W. W. NORTON & COMPANY
New York   London

Plans for Departure

A NOVEL

Nayantara Sahgal

◆

Copyright © 1985 by Nayantara Sahgal
All rights reserved.
Published simultaneously in Canada by Penguin Books Canada Ltd,
2801 John Street, Markham, Ontario L3R 1B4
Printed in the United States of America.

The quotation on pp. 24–25 is based on Dadabhai Naoroji's
presidential address to the second session of the
Indian National Congress.
The quotation on p. 46 is from the Brhadaranyaka, believed
to be the oldest of the Upanishads.
The quotation on p. 173 is from Rudyard Kipling's poem
"The White Man's Burden."

The text of this book is composed in Trump Mediaeval,
with display type set in Trump Mediaeval.
Composition and manufacturing by
the Maple-Vail Book Manufacturing Group.
Book design by Judith Henry.

First Edition

Library of Congress Cataloging in Publication Data
Sahgal, Nayantara, 1927. Plans for departure.
I. Title.
PR9499.3.S154P5   1985   823   85-3037
ISBN 0-393-02221-8
W. W. Norton & Company, Inc.
500 Fifth Avenue,
New York, N.Y. 10110
W. W. Norton & Company Ltd.
37 Great Russell Street,
London WC1B 3NU

1 2 3 4 5 6 7 8 9 0

For Premilla Menon,
companion in laughter

PLANS FOR DEPARTURE

O   N   E

"What is this supposed to be?" demanded Sir Nitin
Basu, poking at the lumpy cutlet on his plate.
He cared less about the lump's name than
why it was being served to him at all. He might be getting
old but he wasn't ailing, and it was insulting to a sophisticated palate to be fed saltless dollops of boiled meat.

"Fricadella is the name of it. It is Danish. I hope you like
it, Sir Basu."

He had been afraid it was Danish, synonymous for him
with outlandish. Miss Anna Hansen sat opposite him at
the small round dining table, her figure uncannily erect, if
you could call such unflinchingly straight elongated lines
a female figure. She was eating a curious-looking concoction of nasturtium seeds, mint, and unidentifiable leaves
and grasses, which she was welcome to punish herself with
provided she left his diet alone.

"I try to think of new meat dishes," she said.

"Don't think of new dishes, Miss Hansen. I prefer the
ones I am used to, and as you are practically a vegetarian
yourself, there is really no need for you to trouble with
meat."

Or to trouble with menus at all, since food was not what
she was here to attend to and he had politely told her so
once a week, in other words, twice since her arrival.

"It is no trouble at all," she protested.

Eyes as glacially gray-blue as the northern hemisphere's sun-starved skies looked pleasantly back at him. She could have been any age between thirty-one and ninety-one as far as he was concerned. Long Hindu habit always made Sir Nitin add one to a round number. Twenty-one rupees to nieces and nephews on their birthdays, a hundred and one for weddings, fifty-one to charities. The odd number was considered auspicious. His own use of it for gift-giving was a sparse concession to the quirks of his ancestors, in an otherwise Reformed upbringing that had lived cheek by jowl with Christianity too long to remain orthodox, or, heaven forbid, superstitious.

He was no good at guessing human ages. His skilled and patient looking was done through a microscope. Miss Hansen's age was as indecipherable as hieroglyphics, her coloring as foreign as fricadella to his palate. He knew nothing about women, and her fine, pale hair and ice-blue eyes gave him no clues. Her teeth and bones were splendid, her energy unsurpassable. But if anyone had asked him whether she was attractive or plain, he would not have known what to say. The sheer foreignness of her appearance—that whitish hair, those limbs—exceeded even that of the English. It was impossible to make judgments about anything so remote from what usually met the eye.

He had engaged Miss Anna Hansen to take dictation and help him get his jungle of papers in order, not as the housekeeper and general busybody she had insisted on becoming. He had not, in fact, engaged her. His sister, who had taken the task upon herself, had sent her here, and it had never occurred to Sir Nitin until he set his astonished eyes on Miss Hansen—the letter announcing her date of arrival having got here after her—that Didi's choice would be

European and female. He had naturally been expecting a man, a *babu* accustomed to clerical work, with a proper if unintelligible command of English. If by some freak mischance his assistant was to be a woman (except that the thought had never crossed his mind) then Didi should have had the sense to engage an Indian Christian widow. He was filled with a yearning for her now, someone pious and convent trained, proficient at note taking, and grateful to eat what the cook could provide. She would have been a matron of recognizable matronly shape, in straitened circumstances, and of an age and stage in life not to be compromised by living under his roof. With Miss Hansen's age a puzzle, he could not be sure if her presence was causing comment. And what on earth would she do with her spare time? Himapur had no social life to speak of, certainly none requiring elaborate changes of clothes. Henry Brewster, the District Magistrate, was practically the sum total of officialdom here, and protocol was not his strong point. Most of the Europeans Sir Nitin knew took part in organized sport and changed their clothes several times a day. The two weeks of Miss Hansen's stay had not reassured him about the problem of how she would spend her spare time. She simply took off when her work was done, for hours at a time.

The Indian Christian would have gone to church on Sundays and would almost certainly have involved herself with the newly founded mission's activities. Miss Hansen showed no sign of religion. He had never seen her so much as bow her head. He found it very disconcerting, a kind of blow aimed at the Christian-Western influences that had hovered about his Hindu family ever since he could remember, and made modern, enlightened Indians of them—except Didi, who remained unrepentantly riddled with superstition. Miss Hansen could have been a spirit—if anyone so athletic and vigorous could be called a spirit—out of an Old Norse saga. For a man who had never had any woman other than his kith and kin under his roof, her presence was as alarming as invasion. Her absences alarmed him even more, headed as she always was for no known destination.

Didi had tried for years after their parents died to arrange a marriage for him, but when he had finished getting degrees he had plunged into experiments in plant tissue, and by the time he had looked up from them long enough to notice the date, time, and year in the world outside botanical science it was too late. The eligibles had disappeared into matrimony and motherhood. There remained the possibility of a lady lawyer or a lady doctor, one of a trickle the last decade of the old century had ushered in. Such a bride would have been fairly advanced in years, certainly past thirty. She would have been a professional female with an anatomy and disposition to match. The very idea had so intimidated him, he had begged Didi to give up her search, and she had reluctantly contented herself with bossing and fussing over him from afar. She and her husband lived in Calcutta. He, until he had come here to Himapur, had taught at the University of Allahabad. Suddenly recognition, knighthood, and distinction had descended on him and he had fled from the publicity, giving himself a June to September respite away from teaching.

"I shall not be needing you this afternoon, Miss Hansen," he said.

"So! I take a walk to the shops."

Miss Hansen lived perpetually in the present. He was tired of changing her *s*'s to *ed*'s in the notes she made for him in her spikey, continental handwriting, so unlike the script of the English or the round, clear hand of the convent-trained Indian.

In the fortnight since she had been in his employ, he had got used to her six-mile walks, three to the shops—as the ranshackle sheds under corrugated iron roofs on the mall were known—and three back. "I can not see me carried by dandy upon the shoulders of those poor, thin coolies with their caving-in chests. So also I can not sit in a rickshaw bursting their lungs out getting me up the hill," she had said when he had told her about the mode of transport in the hills. It was an admirable sentiment, and neither could *he* picture her athletic form daintily conveyed miles up and downhill. But what other way was there to travel? Everyone used dandies and rickshaws, and no adult he knew was thinner than a coolie. Her striding about made her even more conspicuous than she already was. Her comings and goings had put his cottage on the map, a publicity he shrank from and had come all the way here from the plains to escape, apart from needing the time to collect his thoughts for the next phase of his work. In an incomprehensible discourse he had listened to with one ear, so busy had he been trying to chew and swallow some tasteless specialty better suited to Danish teeth and palates, she had gone on at great length about the plight of the coolie. Something to do with malarial swamps, and hungry lions taking a dreadful toll of coolie lives in some region of Africa.

"Is there anything you need from the mall, Sir Basu?"

"The correct form is Sir Nitin," he pointed out, not for the first time.

"Yes, and meaningless like some of the English ways," she said cheerfully. "So also is the English spelling."

No Indian woman sat so straight. They leaned, they slumped, they dipped and arched. They ducked their heads.

Without exception they ducked their heads. Womanliness was composed of that sort of tuck and turn and sideward posture, though in his student days in Victorian England he had seen English ladies ramrod straight, a proud bearing most triumphantly embodied in Victoria's daughter-in-law, Princess May, now Queen Mary—a carriage that represented the empire itself, its discipline, its standards. But it was achieved, as was well known, with backboard practice for growing bones, and whalebone corsets in maturity. Corsetry was an inescapable fact of posture. Yet Miss Hansen had posture without aids. This was clear from her freedom of movement, they way she set her feet squarely upon the ground, the distance she covered in a single stride—disturbing indicators of an unsupervised upbringing.

How like Didi not to check her antecedents. If he had not been so engrossed in his life's work he might well have gone into the history of Miss Anna Hansen. Why was she here at all? Why had she journeyed from Denmark to India, and, apparently hearing from mutual friends in Calcutta of his need, applied to his sister for the job, which his sister in a fit of temporary insanity or early senility had given her, blithely sending her twelve hundred miles northwestward by train, and then, by horse-drawn tonga, eight clip-clop miles a day to Himapur. Unlike more accessible hill stations, it was not blessed with a mountain railway. She now sat, an eccentric spinster, immensely tall—compared with himself and the cook, who were the only other human beings for at least five furlongs—across the table from him, where the Indian Christian would never have dreamed of parking herself. She would have eaten separately and unobtrusively of whatever the cook prepared and retired early, leaving him to himself at the end of the day. Not so Miss Hansen, who was under the impression he needed her company. In the evenings she cast a huge shadow. He supposed her height was why she had never married, though where there were women as high as elms, there must be men like oaks. Not that Miss Hansen was not womanly in other ways. She knitted—but with her knitting held well above the book in her lap which she went on reading. And if she was not reading, she looked out of the window or around the room, everywhere but at her knitting. And her knitting did not take the soothing conventional form. It was some abbreviated technique that got done twice as fast due to the shortcut, but which deprived it of the graceful gradual motions that made knitting so womanly an occupation. The Danish style, he supposed.

"The Danish queen goes on her bicycle to buy vegetables," Miss Hansen said, and he realized she had just remarked how useful a bicycle would be up here. "She hangs her shopping basket on the handle."

For the life of him he could not imagine Queen Mary, Empress of India, shopping for her own potatoes on a bicycle with a basket hanging from the handle. He wondered if coming from a people whose queens went shopping on bicycles and kings played tennis in their nineties had something to do with the unsettling effect of Miss Hansen. He swallowed the last of the cutlet known as fricadella. He had no intention of ever eating one again. The cook, a young hillman, came in with two bowls of unpeeled, sliced fruit and set them down. Sir Nitin looked at them in profound disbelief. He had a sweet tooth and the cook knew it. The luscious *rasagolla*, the chaste *sandesh*, the fattening delicacies of his childhood, his youth, and his dreams, were not available here, but anything, anything containing a generous helping of sugar would have comforted him at the close of this frugal meal. Instead he was presented with bleak, unskinned apples and pears. The post arrived in the middle of the fruit, giving him the excuse to push his bowl aside and open the letter he had taken from the cook. It was from his sister.

"By this time," he read, "Miss Anna Hansen will be well settled into her duties. I can hardly believe my good fortune in finding her. So ideal. And Europeans are so much more efficient than us. She will be a godsend to you. But apart from that, Potla"—Sir Nitin was sixty and his sister sixty-five, but they still called each other Big Sister and Bundle—"she is the best type of European. I am told she has studied our history and culture at Adyar and is very interested in Hindu doctrines, which means in religious matters she must be a freethinker. I don't know what possesses you to buzz off to Himapur of all dreary places, and then in the off-season when there won't be a soul to talk to, but she will be the perfect companion for you in your isolation. I am told she cooks and sews and knits as well." Miss Hansen, it was plain, had been hired on some lunatic's hearsay, though Didi must have interviewed her, and therefore set eyes on her, and still sent her here regardless. It could not even be put down to change-of-life confusion. Didi had five grandchildren and was long past change of life.

Miss Hansen finished her fruit and stood up. "Now I leave."

He was still reading Didi's long, rambling, patronizing letter when he saw her go past the dining room window looking like a Russian peasant with her headkerchief tied under her chin. She carried no raincoat or umbrella. The Indian Christian would have carried both and a woolly as well because quite obviously the day was dark, dank, damp, and miserable. A moment later a thrilling, heart-stirring whistle pierced the air. It was unbearably, hauntingly sweet, impaling him to his chair. It vibrated into a lyrical, accurate rendering of Mendelsohn's "Spring Song," the flight of the melody as startling as that of a rare, rich-plumaged bird, as unexpected as pure joy. The whistle faded, leaving him peculiarly shaken. He looked at the pines framed in the window, and the woods beyond. Mist swirled into the dining room until a thick, impenetrable curtain of it hung between him and the pines.

Anna climbed the steep slope energetically and, ignoring the main road used by rickshaws, dandies, and sedate walkers to the mall, she stepped up to a footpath above it and turned left. The footpath went both right and left, encircling the hill like a loose, uneven girdle around bulging hips, its two ends losing themselves before they could meet hours later on the other side where the forest died a sudden death. What was left of the track fell steeply into a gorge. Huge boulders barred the way beyond it like prehistoric citadels. There was no traffic between the green hills of Himapur and the barren mountains of the interior. The desolate grandeur of the snow range looming above them looked cosy by comparison. Leftward, anyway, took her and the occasional, jogging mail carrier she met on her rambles, to the mall.

A few yards along her path the deodar forest closed around her and heaved a heavy, restless sigh. She glanced up through treetops at patches of tarnished sky to see clouds hurrying urgently toward her. In places the path was so narrow she had to squeeze past the hillside, taking care not to disturb the pouches of mist lodged in its hollows and crevices. Vertical meadows of ferns rose in banks above her. Flocks of them lined her path. She lifted her skirt to prevent it from brushing the rain off them. An abundance of fragile maidenhair rippled toward her, and other coarser aromatic varieties bristled and beckoned from their clusters, her favorites the silver-backed beauties she sometimes took home to put in a vase. She rounded a curve to find crocuses growing wild on the bank above and below her. A patch of purple shade turned out to be violets. To say the least, it was confusing to find so much of Europe here, the trees most familiar of all, pines, oaks, spruce, chestnuts. She had to close her eyes to remember she was in India, open them and she was in the Alps. This hill was flanked by higher and lower hills and valleys. Anna could see stone-terraced land on the opposite hillside, densely planted with young, green grain and mortarless houses that she had been told held fast against avalanches. No sunlight flashed off their red and green roofs today.

Released from the conscious effort of English, Anna's thoughts became fluent, doing conjurors' tricks. The massed dark clouds above her rolled over. Great chariot-wheel formations of them raced toward her. The people of the valley, used to the slow ox and the lumbering ass, must have been paralyzed in their tracks as the attacker from the northwest bore down on them, all flying hoofs, flaring nostrils, and a mouth wide open in a laugh like a neigh that was shattering as the sky's thunder. A fusion of chariot, beast, and rider, multiplying as it came, had driven across the sky, torn it apart and rushed like a storm through the gap. Anna knew in every pore what the Indo-Aryan invasion must have been like for those who had lived here in those undocumented times.

The bazaar on the mall reeked of jaggery and *biri* smoke, and the acrid odor of the tattered jute sacking the coolies wore. They squatted outside the rickshaw shed, passing a communal *biri* around and inhaling it deeply through cupped hands. The trestle tables outside the tea shack were empty. The swarm of flies that feasted on the tray of hard brown candy near the kettle were in hiding waiting for better weather. Nor were people much in evidence with rain threatening. Further along, a row of shacks sold grain and potatoes, pots and pans, candles, kerosene, and dusty packets of Britannia biscuits and Cadbury's chocolate. A train of mules was being unloaded in a warehouse at the end of the mall. Mrs. Croft, in long sleeves, a high neck and two felt hats, one fitted into the other (so necessary for proper protection against sun and rain, Anna had heard her say), was in the chemist's, demanding cough mixture as Anna entered. Madhav Rao, though not bundled, wore a crumpled muffler and was sniffling, more out of the sense of importance it gave him, like wearing glasses, than because he had a cold.

"Good afternoon, Miss Hansen," said the missionary's wife. "You don't look prepared for the weather."

"You think so?"

Later, after the evening prayer in the mission compound, Lucille Croft told her husband it wasn't as if Miss Hansen didn't know English. She was just taking advantage. And Marlowe replied seriously, as if he meant it, and she knew he did, compulsive truthteller that he was, "We are not called upon to judge others, Lulu." But if they were not called upon to judge others, what were they doing saving souls in this back-of-beyond instead of staying on in Calcutta with a church and a respectable congregation whose reactions you could tell, unlike the locked and barred faces at prayers in the mission compound? She was already tired of being marooned without her own kind for company, except the District Magistrate and summer visitors who left as soon as the rains began. Marlowe was right when he said the Word of God was more needed here than in Calcutta. She wished it was more welcome. With every panting coolie breath and low muttered chant that took her rickshaw up and down the hilly roads she distinctly sensed hostility, much more of it than their wiry little bodies should be able to contain. She sensed it even when they jog-trotted comfortably enough on level ground, when with a hoarse coolie version of Hoop-la they swung without warning into a fast gallop sending her slithering on the leather seat till she balanced. It could be her imagination, a thing she was gifted with and Marlowe wasn't, that the Lord's work was being resisted by even the coolies' legs, when their corded tendons jutted angrily as they dragged the rickshaw uphill, or by the determined backward slant of their bodies as they heaved and strained the other way to prevent it from sliding out of control. She had to push herself hard against the back of the seat and hang on to the hand rails to keep herself from skidding off and landing in the *khud*. If they had their way that's where they'd like to see her. "Now why would they want to do that, Lulu?" was Marlow's mystified comment.

Lulu noticed Miss Hansen was not buying anything. She was having an endless chat with the shopkeeper, delaying the cough mixture, and his oily-haired children were prancing around her. And chatting about what, may I ask, but are the flowers screaming nicely today, Tantanna, and yes, thank-you, they are screaming nicely today. If Lulu hadn't heard it herself she would have said the two of them were off their rockers. If God had wanted flowers to scream, their screams would have been hearable by everybody, and an English scientist would have made the discovery through proper English science. And Tantanna, if you please! If that was any kind of name at all, was it necessary to let the shopman get so familiar?

"Her name is Anna, Lulu," her husband said, as if she didn't know, after the prayer meeting.

"The point is I distinctly heard her being called Tantanna by the shopman and his children. I don't know what she thinks she's up to, working for a so-called scientist and being called Tantanna by every Tom, Dick, and Harry. Can't you get her to come to services? It'll look very odd if we can't even get a Christian to come."

In any case they were hard up for anything remotely resembling a decent-sized congregation. Who wanted to come to sermons when there was no church, and the District Magistrate was sitting tight on their request for a site to build a church, taking his sweet time about it. She had to admit, with one Englishman in charge of everything from law and order to land, water, roads, and taxes, and disputes about all of them, things took time, but not this long. And Marlowe, whose self-assurance was as mesmerising as her father's, waited about, meek as a lamb, for the D.M. to take action instead of making use of his natural authority as he had done with her father. She had never been aware of disputes on her father's plantation. They had been so easily settled by hired toughs while the District Magistrate there, and all his successors, dithered about the law. Her father had always said he would never have got any indigo planted if he had pampered his workers and waited for penpushers to decide rights and wrongs. She remembered routine thrashings, from her perch on the saddle in front of him. "Right then, get on with the sowing," he'd say when it was over. He would flick his whip against the horse's hindquarters, turn it around and canter it home, while she swerved around on her perch, tickled pink when he wiggled his ears and moved his forehead up and down, clowning all the way home. Life had been simple until the morning Marlowe had barged in with the audacity to confront her father about a decaying corpse. She and her father had never been the same since, though Marlowe hadn't changed a bit. Miss Hansen was handing out toffees to the shopkeeper's greasy children. Lulu rapped on the counter in a businesslike way and Madhav Rao stopped wasting time and came to serve her.

A strong whiff of jaggery announced Miss Hansen's return. Sir Nitin shuddered. More changes in diet. Dirty bazaar jaggery instead of pure white refined sugar. He would have to have it out with her soon or his energies would be spent fuming over food instead of getting the most out of his free time. He was sorting personal papers when she came into his study with a tea tray the cook should have brought, and he told her about the dinner invitation for next week at the District Magistrate's, an evening he would have looked forward to if the Crofts had not been invited too. He had nothing against the missionary, he told Miss Hansen, but Mrs. Croft had been a most unfortunate choice as his wife. Rude. Ignorant. The last time he had met her she had had the temerity to question his family's loyalty to the Crown. She went too far. He had been one of the youngest men present at the founding of the Indian National Congress.

When Miss Hansen had left him to drink his tea in peace, he tried to recall his speech on the occasion. It came to him with the relaxed ease of school Shakespeare and biblical psalms. He had memorized and rehearsed it with actions in front of his bathroom mirror. He could see himself delivering it in Bombay that December morning in 1885, as dignified as any of the older men present, and much better dressed than most of them in his morning coat and striped trousers:

Is this Congress a nursery for sedition and rebellion against the British Government? (cries of "no, no"); or

is it another stone in the foundation of the stability of
that Government? (cries of "yes, yes"). Let us speak
out like men and proclaim that we are loyal to the
backbone (cheers) . . . that we thoroughly appreciate
the education that has been given to us, the new light
which has been poured upon us, turning us from the
darkness of Asiatic despotism to the light of free English
civilization. (Resounding cheers.)

His work had kept him free of political involvement. A
lucky escape considering the convulsions the Congress was
going through. Before his arrest Tilak had tried to turn it
into a platform for agitation. "Don't talk to me about half
loaves and whole loaves," he had declared in a speech that
was a disgrace to the organization's high oratorical standards, "I want the whole loaf and I want it now." He said
he believed in passive resistance and called his strategy
boycott, but every time he opened his mouth, someone else
got ready to throw a bomb. When he made it clear the government did not suit him, it was certain not to suit a few
thousand others as well, bomb throwers among them. He
had only to defy the chairman at the 1907 session and insist
on speaking for the meeting to end in an uproar. Sir Nitin
had felt duty-bound to attend it. The chairman of the
reception committee had privately appealed to all moderates to be present. Tilak had stood defiant on the dais, his
arms crossed, while pro- and anti-Tilak militants bran-
dished sticks and hurled sundry missiles at each other across
the delegates' heads, and as the place rapidly emptied of
speakers and audience, they proceeded to charge around
like maniacs, breaking up the furniture. Walking out with
as much haste as dignity would allow the minute a shoe
sailed past his ear, Sir Nitin had heard a voice behind him
say with a cool, dry precision more chilling than hysteria,

"Well at least we won't go to our graves passing resolutions and signing petitions."

"You do see why we had to deport him," Robert Pryor, new Home Secretary, United Provinces, had said at a select private dinner soon after his appointment, explaining Tilak's six-year prison sentence under the Newspaper (Incitement to Offences) Act.

Sir Nitin saw.

This part of the house served as his office. A glass-fronted enclosure extended the villa westward by eighteen feet. Long, lingering sunsets stained the sky scarlet through the trees. Henry could no longer see the forest through the sheet glass, only his own shadowy lamp-lit reflection in it, but during daylight it reminded him he had been posted to Himapur because it had more pine and deodar woods than human habitation. Written and unwritten rules did not apply to trees. Trees did not rise up and mutiny, prattle about Home Rule or throw bombs. A District Magistrate could confer with them without endangering the empire, and his superiors could rest easy.

The gaudy bucaneering days of Company Bahadur had at least breathed life instead of rules, he thought. Those were the days of private armies and private fortunes out of plunder and loot, of mingling and mistressing, and hail fellow well or ill met, when crass commerce had ruled the roost. Then came the Mutiny and goodbye to all that. A state of emergency had come to stay, and British social life had retreated behind fortifications. A servant of the Crown who had other ideas was better off tucked away where he need not be exposed to temptation. Henry's posting to Himapur implied that said servant of the Crown, eminently worthy in other ways, had an annoying tendency to keep making a case for the fox. Himapur was not a punishment. It was, in fact, a favor to anyone who had had malaria five times, suffered from philosophy, and had chronic attacks of ruling-class conscience. A ridge in the Himalayan foothills bordering Nepal that had been British by right of conquest for ninety-nine years, and where nothing had happened since then that could cause the slightest nervous tremor at the provincial capital, was the perfect place for recovery. But, of course, the opposite had proved true. Time and thought were a lethal combination. His benefactors should have known that on borders reason and law had a way of becoming what every man made for himself. Narrow valleys at the foot of high mountains were not immune from dreams and desires, or Sarajeveo would not have become the scene of the world's must publicized crime.

The letter on his desk, from the Home Secretary to the government of the United Provinces, called it "a sign of the times" that since last writing he had to alert Henry about another resident, besides the missionary, on whom he hoped Henry was keeping a routine eye. Robert Pryor must have slept bolt upright and alert if he slept at all. His letter made Henry's harmless list of four guests for dinner exactly fifty percent suspect by the prevailing standards of hypertension and suspicion. According to Pryor, the Valkyrie, who tramped the hillside in seven-league boots, judging by the amount of territory she covered on a walk, needed watching because she had spent several months after her arrival in India at the Theosophical Society in Adyar in the south. In a note attached to his official letter Pryor's plump little fingers had sketched out much more background than he need have to a district officer—a mark of his continuing special interest in Henry, and not just scoutmaster technique to chivvy up a slow coach whose eyes did not glaze and shine instantly at mention of king and country. The Society, he wrote, had been the scene of some very peculiar goings-on since its founding in New York in 1875, with the backing of an American Santa Claus. Its leading light was a Russian noblewoman, Countess Helena Petrovna Blavatsky—bogus as they come—who claimed to have had mystical experiences in Tibet. More likely she was a spy. She had written two preposterous books, *Isis Unveiled* and *The Secret Doctrine,* putting Christianity on a level with Greek myth and Eastern superstition—as if there were actually some basis for comparison. Mrs. Besant had become head of the Adyar branch after the Blavatsky woman and she, of course, was up to her English ears in Hinduism and national politics.

All sorts of wild-eyed theories of reincarnation are being bandied about by this crowd. And if you ask me why we bother about any of this poppycock, it is because religion and culture have become a cloak for danger-ous extremism. Tilak was released last week and got a hero's welcome. I suppose you know the cloth, freight, and share markets in Bombay shut down when he was arrested, which shows he had the support of wealthy Indian merchants and financiers, apart from the mill-hands who went on strike. Fortunately there was no general strike, a method that the violent party in Rus-sia is advocating. If Tilak and his hotheads get control of the Congress, some little event could trigger a native uprising. He's got the Irish disease and is hell bent on Home Rule. He writes like a rabble-rouser. It's hard to believe he was a professor before he took to inflam-matory journalism.

All roads—religion, culture, and the hereafter—led to Pryor's next unerring emphasis: "Don't lose sight of the fact these are a violent people," followed, oddly enough, by: "We have won India by the sword. I hope the tiny educated class which the Congress represents, will have the intelligence to realize its best hope is with us, and that the British sword stands between it and the rest of the native population." Pryor ended with: "Terrorist activity is on the wane, but not nearly fast enough considering the partition of Bengal was annulled three years ago." And, as if Henry needed a reminder, "You are well out of it, my dear Henry." But even Pryor, constantly threatened by chaos, and carried away by his allergy to the bogus Blavatsky and her Tibetan transports, must know his warnings had nothing to do with a single-minded missionary, whatever his record, and a marathon walker. Her hilarious English and zero knowledge of native tongues would confound any subversive design even if the populace was pining to be subverted. From what he had seen of Himapur's inhabitants they were too busy scratching a living. And settlers from the plains were too far from the plains to catch any political contagion.

Henry got up and drew the curtains across the dark glass expanse. The room gained an immediate warmth and intimacy. Proportionately his serenity ebbed. Leisure was upon him. An evening spent with others might carve it into manageable pieces. In the dining room the bearer had folded napkins to look like starched linen swants. Cloudy evenings could be cool and he had had a pine-cone fire lit in the drawing room. He dressed and returned to it in time to hear the minor pandemonium of the Croft arrival. It must be their rickshaw on the gravel because he could hear the Croft female's uneducated voice, but four people erupted into the room together like bad stage management. The other two, Sir Nitin, who was puffing, and the Valkyrie, must have walked. The front door closed on a grumbling murmur. Trust La Croft to irritate and infuriate with an argument about small change. She had a genius for rubbing people the wrong way, and he saw an evening of damage ahead. A woman like her could undo years of good will in five minutes. Planters and missionaries were an administrator's nightmare and the Croft couple was one of each. Nothing could have persuaded Henry that two such diametrically opposed nuisances could ever have got together at any level, much less in matrimony. A marriage of the two was carrying a bizarre experiment too far. If Robert Pryor needed an omen of disaster, it was much more likely to be lurking in this unlikely couple than in Tilak, who, after all, would only hasten history. He remembered to greet the walkers first as befitted Sir Nitin's knighthood and status, and signaled for a whiskey and soda which his most important guest accepted gratefully. The Valkyrie took a sherry, with the innocent enthusiasm of a child of twelve tasting one for the first time.

"Trouble with your rickshaw pullers?" Henry asked Marlowe Croft.

La Croft replied instead. "The noise they make about it when they know very well that everything in this part of the world comes on a man's back. At least they're pulling a rickshaw, not carrying it. Good evening, Mr. Brewster."

"Or muleback," Henry reminded her, summoning a smile and shaking her hand, a ridiculous custom originating from having to find out whether the other fellow was concealing a weapon, which La Croft might well have been doing.

"Mrs. Croft is not heavy, but I'm quite a weight," said Marlowe Croft, stating the obvious. "I always walk, but I hurt my ankle today and gave in to the temptation to ride. All heavy stuff comes on mules, Lulu, so maybe you and I should."

"It's wicked the fuss they make. One of these days they'll slip on purpose to land me in the *khud*," said La Croft.

She took off her raincoat and her hats. In the drawing room she took the sherry her husband had refused, treating the D.M.'s house as "her" territory, not subject to mission rules. Croft stood his ground near the door.

"I believe I should go out and pay those men some extra money," he said.

Henry said his servant would do so but the missionary would not hear of it. The other three sat down looking ready for skirmishes, if not outright battle, and showed no sign of wanting to be sociable even about the weather. There was no excuse for all this wariness since they had met before, though it was the first time they had assembled here, and a more unmixable bunch would take some finding. Quite unnecessarily the Valkyrie revived the coolie controversy with "Loads they can carry, or how was the Uganda railroad so heroically completed in nineteen-oh-one."

La Croft looked dazed but Sir Nitin corrected, "Those were not *these* coolies, Miss Hansen. The men you are talking about were indentured laborers. They happen to be known as coolies in Africa, but they are not what *we* call coolies."

"Those and these," the Valkyrie shrugged. "From my reading I know they carry six hundred miles of iron to lay tracks over dangerous country."

Dispensing salted nuts, Henry remarked soothingly, "You're referring to the Uganda railroad—a venture that cost the British six million pounds."

A polite monosyllable or two dropped shallowly into the vacuum. The Valkyrie declared herself opposed to exploitation. Marlowe Croft, who had returned, sat silent as the tomb.

"You must settle a question for us, Miss Hansen," La Corft set her own little ball rolling, half her sherry inside her. "I distinctly heard you being called Tantanna yesterday afternoon. That couldn't be your name, and a shopkeeper would hardly be using a *nickname*, I told Marlowe, or even a *Christian* name without a Miss before it."

"I do not like the Miss before," the Valkyrie cordially replied. "I look after children before coming here and I always ask them to call me Tante Anna for Aunt Anna. So everyone does. And in Denmark there is no difference between the shopkeeper."

"Dear me," said La Croft, putting an end to that line of discussion.

The fire leapt, the pine cones in it hissed and spat like a nasty-tempered orange and black cat Stella had once had. It was the only sound in the room until Henry took matters in hand and asked Sir Nitin how his work was getting on. But this time the Valkyrie with stars in her eyes explained unasked that Sir Basu's work is about the unity of life, would you not say so, Sir Basu, making "Sir Basu" look exceedingly put out. So there must be some mild friction in that camp, too, and no wonder. Henry doubted whether he himself could have had such a very definite personality as the Valkyrie underfoot day in and day out, even though he was more of a match for her in height, build, and color, which, according to the government's unwritten law, was supposed to lay the foundation for Pax Britannica, or at least for harmonious lunch and dinner get-togethers.

Sir Nitin, who hated amateur inanities about serious subjects, recognized Henry's real interest and grudgingly relented under the spell of his life's work.

"You might call it that," he said, "And there is good reason to when we know, for example, that plants react to time just as animals do, or we ourselves. Leaves change their position by day and night, even when light and dark are artificially regulated. And sea anemones have a way of expanding and contracting to the rhythm of tides, as I am sure you are aware."

No one was. But Croft decided to be neighborly and remark, "Is *that* right?"

"Oh yes. They go on doing so for some time even if they are taken out of their natural habitat and put into a tank. And there is no question, I am convinced, that plants react to kindness and cruelty. My experiments show that plants feel pain."

La Croft burst into a merry laugh. In the stunned silence everyone waited for her to stop and for Sir Nitin to go on, but it was she who went on, saying these experiments, and you could hear the quotation marks in her tone, must have been done before. In England. A wintry calm descended while a distinguished scientist believed his ears. He retorted frigidly that if they had been, he would hardly have claimed them as his own.

"I just wondered," laughed La Croft.

It was the signal for Sir Nitin to launch straight into a belligerent recital of the striking results of his experiments with vegetable after vegetable. The tough old birds they were having for dinner (called chickens by the cook) instead of tender roast beef because of Sir Nitin, didn't help to lighten the atmosphere. The green peas with them were a calamity. Sir Nitin's account of the violent death suffered by the pea, when cooked to a temperature of 150°F, sent La Croft into fits of giggles. Who would ever believe such a thing! Oh, she didn't mean any offense, she said, subdued by her husband's expressionless stare, and it might be the sherry she wasn't used to that put the lid on it when Mr.— she meant *Sir*—Nitin Basu said a dying pea went through agonies the same as if a man was popped into a pot and brought to a rolling boil.

"I guess what Mrs. Croft means," remarked Croft, "is that putting us humans in the same boat with vegetables sounds unacceptable to some of us. With due respect I have to agree with Mrs. Croft."

What Croft guessed was beside the point. Henry heard echoes of another farcical conversation around this candle-lit dinner table.

Anna sat facing the sideboard with the picture above it. When she concentrated on it above Lulu Croft's wounding chatter, it turned out to be a series of photographs of a lady and a little girl, taken one after another on the same occasion, arranged sequentially in a single frame. Up in the top left corner the lady sat on a bench under a tree on an agreeable sunny day. The snow-covered mountain behind her, narrowing like a spire, showed the picture had been taken here, in the garden outside. Sunrays filtered through branches to brighten a head of billowing dark hair—spread over her shoulders to dry?—and touched the dark hair of the little girl in braids and pinafore making daisy chains on the grass at her feet. The top right picture had the lady getting up from the bench, the little girl up, too, trailing her daisy chain along the grass. Bottom right, the lady was kneeling beside the child, her hair tumbling over her arms, explaining something. At bottom left she was walking agitatedly away at quite a pace, with the girl clinging to her hand. Anna's eyes traveled over the frame. The picture jerked into staccato life, and as she repeated the exercise it glided into motion. The two minutes in which it must all have happened were captured, but only just, so quickly must the lady have jumped up, whispered to the child and dragged her away before the shutter clicked. The bench must have been empty ever since. Anna forgot about the rest of the dead bird waiting on her plate to be eaten, and put her knife and fork primly side by side as the English did.

She caught her host watching her, a thoughtful look on his sallow face, and said, "It is a feat of photography."

"I took those. The one Madhav Rao, our local photographer-cum-chemist, took of her is dreadful. He's so proud of it, I've never had the heart to tell him so."

"Of her?"

"My wife."

The two words vividly recalled the departure of Stella's luggage caravan. In his mind's eye he could see the last cabin trunk disappear round the bend of the road on muleback, leaving him with a sense of historic defeat. That was how it would be, how they would all leave, bag and baggage, in twenty or thirty years' time, or however long it took for Robert Pryor and company to come up against the question of what they were doing here at all in 1914, so long after the real and rousing relationship had ended. The government should have been planning to phase itself out, and passing acts of conviviality meanwhile, instead of riot acts. Here at table he would have liked to say, Our days are numbered, to see what his unpredictable guests would make of it. Private problems were in a different category, of course, not to be tossed about lightly for comment. So when La Croft enquired, "What do you hear from your wife, Mr. Brewster, and your dear little daughter? They've been away *quite* a time now, haven't they? Gracious, it can't already be nine months, can it?" Henry wanted to pick up his plate, tough bird portion, congealed gravy and all, and hit her on the head with it. She was the sort anyone around the table would take a hatchet to without a qualm.

"The climate didn't suit our daughter," he said, outwardly calm with nine months' practice. "We decided it would be better for Jennie to live with her grandparents and go to school in England. More vegetables, Mrs. Croft?"

She turned to the dish the bearer held at her elbow.

"Not after what we've been hearing, thank-you. Oh, but it's a lovely climate up here and Mrs. Brewster and the little girl looked in the pink."

The bearer arrived with a rigid cornflour pudding surrounded by stewed pears that had clearly collapsed in agony from unbearable temperatures. Henry gave silent thanks that dinner was nearly over. He need not have La Croft again for months, and someone might have cracked her over the skull by then. Marlowe Croft, at the other end of the table, started to spoon solid chunks of pudding into his mouth as if his life depended on it. It was a fact that the husband of the creature had eaten his way through the evening without saying a single word more than was strictly socially necessary.

"I'm glad you approve of those pictures, Miss Hansen," said Henry. "I'm rather pleased with them myself."

"They are intriguing, very. My thought is, what makes her so quickly jump up and go."

Usually the pointless social drill could be relied on as an anaesthetic—assemble in one room, troop into another for dinner, come back to the first. But tonight's party was beyond rescue. Back in the drawing room for coffee, Henry thought the specter of a European war might mellow and unite his guests. Extraordinary how wars cheered up flagging conversation and morale. But now he was the one saying the brutal things while La Croft and Sir Nitin were discussing the assassination of Archduke Franz Ferdinand like old school chums recalling Founder's Day. A pistol shot had accomplished what the march of science could not.

"My own view," said Henry, "is that Austria will have to make some concessions to the Czechs, Serbs, and Transylvanians, or they will consider it their sacred duty to shoot their way out of the empire."

"The Archduke was so popular with his subjects," reminisced Sir Nitin fondly, ignoring his host.

"I shouldn't judge by the peasants gathered to wave flags of loyalty as he drove by," Henry persisted.

"Oh, I should," said La Croft. "After all, he was heir to the throne. They must have waited hours to see him. The papers said the Archduchess was sitting beside him in the motor car wearing a white dress and a big hat. It's so awful to think she was killed too," leaving them with the impression that the final indignity was to be killed wearing a large hat.

Sir Nitin recalled that Franz Joseph's only son, Rudolph, had committed suicide. His wife, the Empress Elizabeth, had been assassinated by an Italian anarchist. His brother, Maximilian, had been shot against a wall in Mexico. Maximilian's wife had gone mad with grief. And now the dastardly murder of his nephew and heir must be the final, unbearable blow to the aging emperor.

On that happy note, Henry's guests got up to leave.

Marlowe lay in bed with his back to Lulu, as she knelt with her forehead propped against the guilt, praying into it. She never knew when to stop, poor Lulu, whether it was praying or saying the wrong thing. The only time he had seen her speechless was on the sweltering day he first saw her, standing arm-in-arm with her medium-drunk out-of-tune father at a piano, singing, "How I *do* like to be beside the seaside!" while another man banged it out on the piano's ancient yellow keys and the lady of the house flurried and subsided alternately round the room like a wingless sparrow. Her hint of lunch had brought a negative roar from the master. No one in his right mind would have hung around waiting to talk business, but Marlowe had not been in his right mind that morning five years ago and he had been convinced ever since that one's right mind was of no great use except in right-side-up circumstances.

"I've come to get the money, Raju's back pay for the crop. Mr. Firth told me he'd talk about it if I stopped by around this time."

"By? Around this time?" she puzzled, fanning herself. "Whose pay did you say?"

With a rare plunge into diplomacy he changed "the tenant who was beaten to death this morning" to "the man who died this morning on your estate."

"Ah. Well I shouldn't talk to him about it just now, Mr. ——," she waited for him to fill her in, while she tapped a foot in weak automatic time to the seaside.

"My name is Marlowe Croft."

"Is it really?" she said, the puzzle clearing. A feeble smile did its best to enliven her features. "You must be an American. I've noticed they often have surnames for first names. It's very curious. How do you explain it?"

He said he couldn't.

"You were named for a poet."

Marlowe doubted it.

"I used to read poetry."

She gestured to the mantlepiece behind her, and he peered. Six microscopic volumes with faded gold lettering were all but hidden behind dusty artificial roses and a fat Coronation mug. Both poetry and fireplace looked as improbable as if she had assured him she used to be young.

"I shouldn't discuss business this morning, Mr. Croft, it's becoming a bit of a party."

"You mean you're expecting more people? Your husband didn't tell me."

"No, it becomes a party when Kewin comes over. His estate is fifty miles away."

"I hate to interrupt the party but the widow is waiting out there with her father-in-law for the money to buy the wood and stuff for the cremation. A body can putrefy fast on a day like this."

"Are you responsible for the funeral then?" she enquired graciously.

Her husband came over, seaside jollity behind him. "I'll be blunt. I like a man who knows which side he's on. Whose side are you on, Croft?"

They had been over it early in the morning. The planter's buying price for the crop had been much lower than the price arranged with Raju. Marlowe was here to collect the balance. This Firth is not a brutish subhuman specimen, Marlowe told himself, he just looks and acts it. Inside he's got an immortal soul same as the rest of us. He explained that Raju's widow would soon have a decaying corpse on her hands. It was the country's custom to dispose of a dead body before sundown of the same day.

"I don't need any teaching about the country's customs. And if the body is decaying, it'll save her the expense of a funeral. Let Mother Nature go to work. And what's it got to do with you anyway?"

What Marlowe should have been talking about was murder and who should be hanging for it, not back pay. He had reported the killing, but what would come of it was anybody's guess. There were practiced murderers among these men. Their forerunners had organized volunteer hanging parties and enthusiastic execution squads after the Mutiny. As often as not authority did not catch up with their blood sport. Firth was not a big man, but put a man in a planter's shoes and around here he grew big. This one had an army of his own, toughs with clubs and spears to do odd jobs on the plantation. The odd-jobs men were at this very moment seeing to it that Raju's family planted the regulation fifteen per cent of Raju's land with indigo.

"What's it got to do with you anyway?" repeated Firth, "I've dealt with meddlers before, the whole misguided lot from the Viceroy down to the newspapers, and daft district magistrates who thought they could tell me how to run my plantation."

And every word of that was true and famous, for the breed if not the man whose house Marlowe stood in. They were a law unto themselves, threatening local magistrates who tried to interfere on behalf of plantation workers. Fifty years ago they had sponsored abuse in the press against the Viceroy, weak-kneed "Clemency" Canning who had forbidden vengeance on the mutineers. Marlowe was well informed about the territory he trod. Not far from this house two planters had tied a *syce* to a tree and flogged him to death. When the crime was discovered, other planters had donated a thousand pounds for their defense, getting them off with three years' simple imprisonment. They stuck together and rampaged together. Marlowe Croft, with no earthly power interested in saving his skin or helping his cause, must have been at least as daft as a district magistrate to say,

"You have broken your contract with one of your workers. A breach of contract is now a criminal offense."

In the humid silence the piano player's hands pressed random keys, found a braying discord and held it. The girl at the piano had a look of strange excitement and elation.

"Temporary rubbish," retorted Firth. "We'll see what happens after your precious magistrate holds his precious enquiry, thanks to your interference."

The party was over. Open to miracles, Marlowe appealed mutely to Mrs. Firth for an act of courage, but her eyes blinked rapidly and fluttered away to the poets. He knew he would have to leave without the money when Firth put an end to the interview with "Lunch, Myrtle."

"You'll be hearing from me, Mr. Firth," said Marlowe.

But Marlowe heard first, when the state's planters took libel action against him. He spent two months in jail, yet Firth, unable to prevent Lulu's marriage to Marlowe, was probably glued to the dancing edge of madness for the rest of his life.

If Lulu kept on as she was doing, they would not have a friend left. The District Magistrate himself would turn against them and would not grant them a site. As soon as Lulu stopped praying and got into bed, he waited for the night to enfold him, leaving him free to review the problems of creating a Christian church. He saw the future unfolding with crystal clarity.

The day after Henry Brewster's dinner party Anna took the path to the right, more of an adventure than she had anticipated. Her progress was slow and stopped entirely when the track lost itself round a bend where a forested ravine took its place. She looked down in dismay. She would have to descend very cautiously into slippery terrain and make her way around the curve until she saw some sign of the path. She sat down and lowered her legs, groping for a heelhold in the hillside's thick pine-needle cover. Beside her the solid stone projection she was clutching for support began to shake like a loose tooth in her grasp. The ground shifted ominously beneath her feet and gave way, hurtling her downward in a cataract of soil and stones. She picked herself up on a broad sunny ledge, more frightened than battered. Her nerves and judgment were badly frayed, but no bones were broken. A rock jutted formidably above her, blocking her view, but she could not in any case have seen her elusive path from so far below. She heard the distant peaceful sound of a streamlet further down, out of sight, or, by the soft symmetry of it, a water-fall. Too far to go in search of water to wash her scratched arms. Anna stretched out in the shade of the rock. Her ledge had a ragged boundary of flowering shrubs. The perpetual rustle of a forest in motion breathed companionably in time to her own breathing. A tawny light dipped and loped delicately as a lean lioness in and out among the bushes. It was a beautiful day. Oh Nicholas, she rejoiced, it's a day of days. She was filled with a passion for Nicholas, and the beauty of this day. If there was love, two people needed no more, not even each other's constant presence. So was this then reliable, everlasting love?

"Your father had good reason to become a romantic idealist," her favorite aunt Inge had said when Anna had gone to say good-by. "I don't know what reason you have. He was very young when Denmark lost Schleswig-Holstein to the Prussians. When you lose one-third of your country and two-thirds of your population, and your family is drowning in shame and claustrophobia, it is bound to make you otherworldly. No wonder he takes to the woods when he gets restless, and does everything but chain himself to railings for women's suffrage. The Danish Women's Society was tremendously bucked when he jumped up in the audience to cheer after the heroine in that play last year made her clarion call for male virginity, though let me tell you he was no male virgin himself. I have always told your mother, Johannes is a spirit in need of air. So wearing, of course, for the spirit's partner. And now your mother is at a total loss to explain to the other aunts why you are leaving England for India when she had just got them used to your being in England."

So had Sir Basu been at a loss at breakfast this morning over why 1500 B.C., when the known past began with Alexander the Great, and why the past at all when modern India was making great strides under British rule? What did it matter *where* the main route of Indo-Aryan penetration lay once they crossed the Indus and poured into the peninsula, unless one was writing a book about it? As for the Aryans astride their dreaded horses trampling everything in sight, no book he'd read about the obscure beginnings of Indian history had made it leap and bound in that fashion. It was most unscientific.

"You are confusing history and mythology, Miss Hansen."

But it had been such an eerily elemental invasion, she said, who could say where myth ended and history began, whether men or gods had hurled thunderbolts at houses and guardian fortresses? Memory had preserved those images down to the last lightning-struck infant burned to ashes blown far and wide by the winds. And what could be more enduring than memory? What else, so to speak *could* be indefinitely preserved, like flowers frozen at peak freshness in lakes of ice, for the scrutiny of later, more scientific times? It must have been quite an event if a military leader ended up in the pantheon. Indra had been no fiercer than later conquerors, only there had been no one to compare him with. First times are so terrifying. And then the irony of that invasion set it apart. The busy settled people he destroyed were never to know he might have done it all in sport, coming as he did from untamed stock that had not heard of settling down. Brick walls and turrets, grain grown and pounded, bronze and ivory and beads? Whatever for? No, she was not writing a book. She just had a traveler's interest in the scene.

"What is germane to the point," said Sir Nitin, pointedly pouring fine white sugar over the banana he had sliced into his porridge, "is that there was no civilization before the Indo-Aryans. There was nothing for them to find and destroy."

Anna admitted she had made up that part of it. She had no archaeological evidence of a lost race with a love of ornament and a genius for urban planning. There was nothing to signify that the earth's oldest piece of cloth lay neatly folded in a silver jar under the floor of an abandoned house. Neither of them knew then that exquisite geometric cities, buried under forty centuries of debris, were going to be excavated in six years' time northwest of their breakfast, but Anna, at least, had not ruled them out.

Anna sat up. The ascent looked perilously perpendicular and unclimbable. She leaned back against the rock face to think about it and sank into the deepest, softest stillness she had ever known. The voice of a man who had been through sorrow and mastered it said wearily, When I was a child, there used to be birds in these woods. Now no bird sings. And don't think we've stopped killing. We're still at it. I've seen too much of it, I tell you. Even I, a soldier like my grandfather who came with the original conquest, have had enough of this orgy of blood-letting. If it isn't the massacre of the inhabitants to clear more space for ourselves, it's blood sacrifice to appease our bloodthirsty gods. Other reasons apart, it is shockingly wasteful. Look at the cartloads of animals we slaughter to propitiate the gods, including the magnificent chestnut beasts on which we rode to victory. We send out our choicest horses as a challenge to neighboring kingdoms, forcing their kings to pay us homage or fight. If the horses are captured we go to war. If they aren't we bring them back here to the capital and sacrifice them. Either way we've lost them, and made more enemies. It is very stupid, his listener agreed, but our hymn about the sacrifice is quite a hymn. Well, which hymn isn't, came the impatient rejoinder, but the listener, who was a Vedic bore, insisted on droning his favorite chant in imitation of a priestly falsetto:

> Dawn verily is the head of the sacrificial horse.
> The sun is his eye; the wind, his breath;
> The universal sacrificial fire, his open mouth;

If horse sacrifice isn't madness, what is? interrupted the first voice sharply. We're masters here. We've burned and cleaned the jungle, subdued the inhabitants, and settled down to till the soil. It's time to stop fighting and killing and to see our gods for what they are, hard-drinking, warmongering, swaggering fellows, greedy for spells and sacrifices. We've got to get rid of them.

Anna smiled. Who wanted a general, an Indra, a Zeus, or a Thor, once wars were over? Indra had had his day, but what a day it had been! A change in the wind's direction, a shivering branch, a cloud formation could revive Vedic battles. She could see the wild rider recklessly race his three-wheeled chariot across the sky, his hair streaming, his victorious drunken laughter echoing in every gust of wind. The truly discerning traveler might still see the bodies of the slain littering the ground and hear Aryan feasting and roistering that must have sounded as ferocious as battle to the defeated trembling in their hiding places. She could imagine Indra's outrage at being forcibly retired. "*I*, who cleared this land for the Aryan?" But it was easy to see why he had had to be replaced. After that ecstasy of conquest the pendulum had swung. Lawless gods were put away. In their place came laws. And to prove that the conquered have the last word, their own awesome Shiva slipped out of remoter antiquity to embody The Law. The age of asceticism had begun. The world and life in it became flimsy outer garments. The struggle for self-mastery was all that was really real. If that was Hinduism in a nutshell, Anna reflected, it was a pity it had not stayed grand and simple, in the nut. She rose to her feet, brushed herself off and examined her lacerated skin. She started to climb carefully, burrowing for hand and footholds beneath the pine needles.

The vanished path appeared, and half a mile along it she

walked into a conference. The District Magistrate and
Marlowe Croft were lifting their walking sticks in various
directions, surveying the cene. Henry Brewster saw her first,
raised his hat and said, "Very ambitious of you to have
come this way, Miss Hansen. People don't usually. Give
us your advice. Mr. Croft wants this piece of land for his
church. What do you think?"

"A church? In this place?" Anna protested.

"I'd like to build it right here," said Croft. "It's not land
anyone else is after, and it's so deserted, a church might
help to get other activities going."

Henry noticed the Valkyrie looked flushed and bewildered. He had watched her come toward them, her cheeks
red with exertion. But her euphoric glow had nothing to do
with mere exertion. It had struck him that the climate and
scenery did rather go to people's heads after the stupefying
heat of the plains. He remembered a sentence he had read
the night before about the strange sensations of pleasure
you had when you arrived at a hill station. Also something
about throwing yourself on a soft turf bank, and plucking
the first daisy you ever saw out of England. Only the Valkyrie, festooned with twigs and foilage, had not thrown
herself on anything so soft as turf. She had angry welts
along her bare arms and her skirt was torn. She saw his
glance and rolled down her sleeves, to prevent comment.
Quite unnecessary, since Croft hadn't noticed a thing.

"I am here to break new spiritual ground," said Croft,
obviously ready to make a literal start.

"Oh quite," said Henry uneasily.

The whole business of allowing missions entry was
complicated enough without dragging spirituality into it.
A priest in a soutane he could understand, whose job it was
to look after the European community's spiritual welfare.

The church was one more expression of white solidarity, and no doubt the quaking post-Mutiny spirit needed constant repair. Missionaries avid for native souls, lining up Jesus Christ with peasant revolt, as this one had done, were another matter. Croft might have a point, but he was a menace. He had spent two months in a very unpleasant cell for providing evidence of a planter's brutality against workers who refused to grow indigo, and he was under warning to stick to his job or face deportation. But Christian propaganda was his job, and he was sticking to it like a leech. Which put Henry's disapproval on the same side as Croft's loathsome persecuting planter.

"And there is no time to lose," continued Croft, doggedly pursuing his mission. "I am as dedicated to my task as you are to yours, sir."

"I'm sure you are."

Henry wished Croft would stop calling him sir when they were the same sort of age. As for dedication, he could think what he liked. If prayerful patriotism had ever been part of Henry's professional makeup, it had worn thin. Matters of weight and importance had changed places with the least important matters. He would have been delighted to see every existing empire pack up, if by their combined disappearance he could regain an earlier peace of mind and lost enchantment. The churchsite could wait. So could the proposal Pryor was expecting from him for setting up a paper mill with the wealth of spruce at their disposal. Lime deposits and other valuable industrial materials waited too. Keeping business and gospel at bay was official treachery and a waste of time. But no more of a waste of time, Henry had concluded, than holding off insurrection.

"This precipice here would have to be fenced in," said Croft, joining him at the edge, "No need to build a wall.

It's a small, unpretentious church I want to build, a simple wooden structure. There's plenty of timber and it won't take long once we get the go-ahead signal from you."

The policy was to leave the country's religions alone. The late Queen, furious with the tepid draft she had been shown, had put her pen through that bit of the Proclamation and rewritten it herself, leaving no one in any doubt about hands-off. Not that Croft's church would interfere with belief and custom. Nobody would pay the smallest attention to it. But one thing led to another when proselytizing hordes were let in. Croft, brick-red from exposure, had a face resembling graven rock. There was nothing of the religious fanatic about him that Henry could recall noticing before, but in this reddish sunlight he looked as fixed, immovable, and unshakable as the Himalayas. England might leave but Croft was here to stay.

"About the church," murmured Henry, "I can't let you know in a hurry. It's not altogether a matter of individual discretion. I may have to refer it to headquarters."

Croft obligingly understood. Croft could wait. If you were waiting for a Second Coming, all other delays must be minor by comparison. They turned back toward the mall, single file on the overgrown path, Anna between the two men.

"You have a good library of books about India, Mr. Brewster, I hear," she said.

"I have some, yes. Please make use of it. Everyday if you like. There's little enough to do here."

"Thank-you, I will. My English reading is better than my speaking."

On the mall she and Croft parted company with Henry Brewster and went to Madhav Rao's shop. Anna waited while Croft bought castor oil for his constipated cook. She felt she owed him an explanation. It was such a very old country, she had meant, with staggeringly old religions.

Whatever else it needed, it did not need one more religion.

"Now that depends, Miss Hansen, on if you are looking at religion like one more brand of tomato ketchup, and I'd certainly like to discuss the subject with you another time. Right now I have to get back with this castor oil."

After he had gone Anna emptied a pocketful of squashed berries and herbs onto the counter.

"Specimens, Madhav. And I can bring bunches more. Why have you no Indian tonics and medicines in your shop?"

Madhav took off the glasses he wore for status and put them in their case to be returned to his nose for his next important customer.

"I am not a shopkeeper, Tantanna. Get this out of your head. I am a photographer. This dealership for a few items is on the side. My caste does not keep shops."

She ran her eye over the bottles in the glass cupboard behind the counter. Dr. Scott's Bilious & Liver Pills, prepared entirely without any mercurial ingredients; Huxley's Ner-vigor Tonic; Wilkinson's Sarsaparilla, wonderful purifier of the human blood; Robinson's Patent Barley.

"Barley of all things! There is so much. And herbs! I have seen masses of juniper growing."

"You have seen juniper doubtless, but who is buying local anything? Let it be. Am I a shopkeeper? This is not a shop. It is a sideline."

"Such stupid waste," said Anna, referring to the bottles, "taking up room on ships coming out when you can make it all here."

There was no one else in the shop. Madhav went to the door and looked up and down the street. He came back to the counter. "You are for boycott?" he asked tersely.

She had been impressed by the fiery eloquence of boycott arguments in Calcutta.

"I am," she said, "it puts pressure."

Madhav fell into impassioned speech. "When the message went out, in one month alone the import of Manchester cloth fell by forty-two million, four hundred and
ninety-two thousand, five hundred yards. What came before
stayed rotting in warehouses."

"Then why are you keeping all these foreign bottles in
your shop?" asked Anna bewildered.

"I am talking about cloth, Tantanna," he reprimanded
her. "Why are you worrying about the shop? It is not a
shop."

Anna sighed. She would never scale the ramparts and
survey the ramifications that Hinduism had become. There
was no going back to the dazzling simplicity of the nut.

"I have come to see your picture of Mrs. Brewster," she
said.

"Then why did you not say so?" he said crossly.

He took her into the suffocatingly hot, hermetically sealed
studio behind his sideline and shut the door.

"The Camera!" he announced, introducing an enormous
hump in a black shroud on a tripod in the middle of the
room. "It was my father's. You may not be knowing he
was chosen the best provincial photographer by the Bombay Provincial Camera Society. He used to say The Camera
keeps images like the mind, so one day it will take pictures
of the past and future, like the mind."

Anna half-listened, circling The Camera that two or three
coolies must have heaved up the mountain road, and fanning herself with her handkerchief at the very thought.

Opening a rear door leading out of the cavernous gloom,
Madhav shouted for a glass of water. Anna glimpsed a lantern-lit room in a maze of shuttered rooms at the end of a
dark passage. The smell of hot, spluttering mustard oil
blended with unknown chemical odors from the darkroom
adjoining the studio.

"What is in those boxes lined up against the wall?" she asked before the door shut.

"Copies of *Kesari* and *Maratha*, Lokmanya Tilak's two newspapers. *Kesari* means Lion and *Maratha* is the name of his and my community."

He seated her with a glass of water the correct distance from his display and drew aside the room's heavy curtains to let daylight flood two walls covered with pictures of whiskered gentlemen in florid-tinted brocades and turbans, holding swords or canes, and wedding portraits of stern couples seated foursquare, their feet planted flat on ornate carpets, staring accusingly into the camera. A short, agonized search located Stella Brewster in a red plush chair with silver tassels dangling from it. She wore a dress of figured green velvet. Her abundant hair was elaborately coiffed. Pink roses neatly climbed gray Corinthian pillars in the background and through the pillars Anna saw two clouds, a lake, and a swan.

"You have painted over the photograph!" she exclaimed.

"To bring out all that is fundamental to the nature of Mrs. Brewster, her character and dignity. You may see it from closer if you like."

"No, no, there is no need," said Anna, "I see it quite well from here. But I can not tell what she is *like.*"

"Just as you see her there," Madhav assured her. "My eldest son took out all the dark shadows in the photo. They were of no use in showing the character of Mrs. Brewster. I put in everything that was fundamental to her nature, such as the dog."

Then Anna saw the circular photograph of a dog pasted at the side of the painted-over photograph, a pretty brown and white spaniel, its colors clearly marked, and "Juliet" in tiny lettering on its collar.

"Mrs. Brewster cannot be conveyed without that animal," explained Madhav. "It is her constant companion. In another life I would not mind being the dog of an Englishman. The coaxing and flattering, and sending ten times a day to the bazaar for this or that item. Treatment fit for a son-in-law."

"So she took the dog with her, too."

"It goes without saying. What is one dog when there is so much luggage?"

Madhav made it sound final. And a ponderous departure it must have been, with no resemblance to the quick, light creature who had fled her husband's camera in minutes.

Which was more like Stella Brewster, the gypsy under the tree after apple harvest time, who had jumped up impulsively and gone? Or this solemn, brown-eyed woman, official and majestic against red plush and Corinthian pillars, who seemed to be there for all eternity? Were her eyes really brown or had Madhav's eldest son decided brown was more fundamental to the character of Mrs. Brewster? Anna felt confused. Fatigue had caught up with her. Her bruises hurt. Present truths were so tangled. They yielded almost nothing, willingly, to one's gaze. It was easier to deal with the distant past, and even the distant future.

"My father was a clerk in the Public Works Department in Bombay," said Madhav, "but photography was second nature to him. In his previous life he was an artist."

"Are you sure?" asked Anna.

"Oh yes. He saw back. He had inner sight."

"And forward?"

"Oh yes. What is the difference? Past, present, future are not divided. Seen from outside the mind they are one."

"But how did he get outside his mind?" she asked.

"By getting control if it, Tantanna. You must be knowing how a good rider controls his horse."

I really should be able to grasp this, she thought, wrestling mentally with an unruly horse and breaking it in, but left with herself on the horse. More practice left her teetering on a pinpoint on the rim of the cosmos, spectator of planets, stunned by star-strewn spaces, with time ticking remorselessly in her ear. She was still in her mind, and it was informing her that her bruises were turning shades of blue.

"How do you not understand such a daily experience of mystics?" demanded Madhav in mild exasperation, "In the flash of Realization, good, bad, past, future, everything is One. My father became Realized when I was ten years old."

He sounded very like Aunt Inge the last time Anna had met her, even more like Aunt Inge earlier when small Anna fell into a daydream over a treat of *smorrebrod* at Tivoli on a Sunday afternoon, so full of the splendors she had seen, she could hardly eat, and had to be prodded awake. She was very nearly in a groggy daydream now with the lack of oxygen.

"Tantanna, you are here. But why?"

The question pounced, rousing her.

"Maybe to be like my brothers," she said slowly. "They do whatever they please. They have been to university. They go anywhere. They waste money. One of them has a long duel scar! If they stay up all night, get drunk, have fights, nobody thinks it is the end of the world."

"Very natural," he nodded.

"After I read Hinduism," said Anna, "I suddenly say to me, in my next life I hope I am a man. But it is too long to wait, so I set myself free in this life."

Madhav looked astounded. More like the other aunts than Aunt Inge. But unlike them he recovered. Not a leaf stirred randomly, he pointed out. So she had not said anything suddenly to herself. If a leaf could be aware of itself, it would know that its own brief, fluttering existence was part of a tree's life, and not an isolated flutter. Everything from a leaf to a bomb was part of a higher Law working itself out. Khudiram Bose was part of it. Dead at nineteen, he had lived to his full span because he had been born to give his life in service of the motherland. Unfortunately his bomb had killed the wrong people, an English lady and her daughter instead of Mr. Kingsford, the Sessions Judge of Muzzafarpur. Both drove to the European club every evening in identical green carriages drawn by white horses. Khudiram had been sentenced and hanged in our Collector's previous district.

Anna sat up, thoroughly awake. "In Henry Brewster's district?"

"Previous. Six years ago on August 11th. The Collector is not the same since then."

Two police guards with rifles took him up to the execution platform. Khudiram shouted "Vande Mataram" (Hail Motherland) at the top of his voice. The crowd became excited and started to shout "Khudiram Zindabad" (Long live Khudiram) and "British Raj Murabad" (Death to the British Raj). He was smiling when they put the noose round his neck. Afterwards they took his body in procession to the cremation ground, and schools and colleges closed for three days as a mark of respect. His photo was still being sold in bazaars.

It was Henry Brewster whom Anna saw, grim-faced witness to a hanging, his features masking his feelings. But his views on assassination were clear enough during an after-dinner converstion in Himapur six years later.

Madhav said Khudiram's comrade had been executed later. In jail he told the warden he had dreamed for months before the event of being an assassin and committing a political murder. In his dream struggles with the police, he had snatched their rifles from them and broken their heads with the rifle butts. Anna found herself contributing Serbian assassinations, of which Archduke Franz Ferdinand's was only the latest. On a June night in 1903 King Alexander and Queen Draga had been shot in their palace. Then the assassins had rounded up the Queen's brother and some of the King's ministers and killed them all as acts of holy duty against those who kept Serbia in bondage. Very telling how assassins had sprung up like barley and juniper both here and in Serbia, wherever exactly Serbia was, remarked Madhav, but on the whole, boycott was better.

"Oh much better," agreed Anna with relief.

But Madhav was calculating the costs. "Boycotters are not deported to Burma or hanged. An explosion maker is hanged. Intending to make an explosion gets transportation for twenty years or jail for seven. But six years for writing! English judges and English juries have changed. There are few right-thinking English officials now."

The English judge at both his trials had said Tilak's articles were seething with sedition and his journalism was a curse to the country! And both times the European majority in the nine-man jury had returned a verdict of guilty, and the Indians of not guilty.

"Apart from the punishment," Anna returned to explosion-making, "violence is not the answer."

"Tantanna! Your brother has fought in a duel."

"So? What is a duel? Only fun."

"Only for fun he uses arms. But the law does not allow us to bear arms, except Indian Christians. How do you tell me, Tantanna, that in my own country I cannot keep a gun even to kill a tiger that attacks my village? How? Year in and year out the Congress is passing the same resolution: Let us bear arms, give us the right."

He laughed hollowly at the fate of Congress resolutions.

"My community was the most powerful before this Raj. Naturally we are very tense about this insult. On top of that writing is also called an explosion."

At his 1908 trial Tilak had argued his own case though he was unwell and getting on in years. The *Manchester guardian* even wrote afterwards: "Mr. Tilak is fifty-two. He will never return from the penal settlement to which he has been consigned." It was ten o'clock and pouring rain on the night of July 22nd, when the sentence was read. The court room was dimly lit. In the half-dark Tilak stood up to declare he was innocent. But there were higher powers ruling destiny, he said, and it might be the will of Providence that his cause would prosper more by his suffering than by his acquittal. And then they hustled him out through the back door to a special train, thinking that would prevent demonstrations. Little did they realize Bombay's millworkers would go on strike for six days, one day for each year of his sentence. Madhav relapsed into silence while Anna stood outside the Bombay High Court in the monsoon downpour with the thousands who waited in vain for Tilak while he was taken stealthily away.

F O U R

It was eleven o'clock on the morning of May 30, 1913, and they were on their way to the opening of a French exhibition at the Duval Gallery in London when Nicholas suggested they set a wedding date. He was Minister at the British embassy in Paris and had to put in an appearance at the gallery, but they would discuss a date at lunch afterwards. All things are possible in a fog-surrounded motor car with the one you love beside you, and Anna tranquilly agreed. In the interests of lucid exchange they usually spoke French, and marriage had always been discussed in French.

"You haven't forgotten I'll have to go to Copenhagen to ask your father for your hand," he said.

"You are unteachable, Nicholas. My father would be most amazed. I can just see his face! You know how he respects my independence."

"So do I, my darling, but one shouldn't grudge the concessions one has to make to birth and upbringing. Ceremony is part of civilized life. Your mother knows it. So does your enormous network of aunts. I spent half my last visit to Copenhagen calling on them. That's what aunts are for. In fact, I'll ask them for your hand instead. And whatever his views, your father can't possibly approve of your working as a governess for no good reason."

"What else can I work at? Women are not trained for anything except chastity and self-denial."

Nicholas decided there was no time to take that melancholy idea to its conclusion before they reached the gallery, and no necessity as it did not apply to Anna. "Why work at all? You're taking the bread out of some woman's mouth who really needs the job."

"I've thought of that," she conceded, "But something in me keeps saying, 'Well done, Anna!' And besides, what is wrong with teaching children fine French?"

The children who were learning fine French belonged, not by chance, to a couple in the front line of women's emancipation. Mr. Marriot was a valued advisor to the militant suffragettes and had staunch pro-feminist links with Anna's father. Nicholas interrupted their talk to tell the chauffeur where to turn at the intersection.

"I promised to take a look at a painting Pierre wants me to buy," he said, "I hope it's not one of the freakish school he's so taken with. Art seems to have lost all sense of direction. Pierre thinks this particular one will be a worth a fortune in a few years' time. You'll be able to advise me."

Nicholas knew more about art than she did but when in doubt he relied on what he called her acute awareness.

"What will you do with another fortune, Nicholas?"

"I know exactly what I shall do with it," he said thoughtfully.

And that, for the moment, was that, meaning she would hear about his long-term plans when present questions had been dealt with.

"We'll talk about the painting at lunch. There won't be room to swing a cat in the gallery, let alone talk. Pierre has invited a mob."

Some paintings change the course of history, Pierre Duval

began to explain as soon as they arrived and his best champagne had been uncorked and served to them, while his second-best was being readied for his lesser clientele. The gallery filled to the brim and he was borne away, gesticulating, a champagne cork bobbing on the tide. Nicholas's tour of the exhibition was halted every few steps by high, delighted voices demanding why he had not told them he was in London. Pierre's guests, more absorbed in each other's pleats and plumes and tiny gold pencils jotting where to meet again, than in Pierre's freaks, made it easier for Anna to walk around the salon. Admittedly champagne creates its own vision, but she was unprepared for what she saw. The course of history was going to be changed, it seemed, by an endless procession of bottles and violins, and human figures stuck with scraps of old newspaper. She came to Pierre's prize exhibit, a chart of some sort, or a collection of children's building blocks, all brownish-gray oblongs and rectangles that could just as well have been viewed upside down. It could also have been an architect's blueprint, if it had stayed put. But the browns rose challengingly to the surface and the grays shyly retreated. She couldn't say what was so disturbingly dreamlike about ordinary mathematical shapes, and why merely looking made brick houses out of them that she could see all sides of. Paint had never played such tricks on canvas before. She was turning away from it when its planes and angles reassembled and a city sprang into view. Pierre was bobbing steadily toward her, and before the tide carried him southward past her, their eyes met in a glance of complete exultant accord.

"Well?" asked Nicholas at lunch.

The waiter arrived with the menu and after a leisurely exchange of views about veal as opposed to lobster, a celebratory wine was chosen. The order of priorities was fatally clear. Food, drink, and the wedding date, followed by life in a jeweled status quo, and at the end of it, Here lies Anna, beloved wife, who died without having made much effort to live, and nobody noticed the difference, since being a beloved wife was supposed to be reward enough. Whereas her priority was life and freedom first. That was where they ran headlong into each's iron wills. They were well-matched in their determination, and neither side gave way. There was no quarrel about the painting. Anna's warm recommendation and Nicholas's decision to buy it marked their last stop together on a known frontier. Thin ice crackled ahead. Yearnings she hardly understood fought with guilt in her heart. She was not explaining herself very well or doing Nicholas justice. She longed to go away and weep wildly before giving him an answer, unless he, normally a shrewd judge of her emotional temperature, kept off the subject. But Nicholas had no intention of keeping off it, or of pandering to her ups and downs today, nor she of deserting her voices. They battled it out in a cold, humorless fury.

"I don't have to marry again," he pointed out, "and you don't have to marry at all. I thought we wanted to."

Anna said she did, but she was thinking of traveling first, and not to anywhere small and Swiss.

"Good God, what for?" said Nicholas, who had seen all of Europe and most British-ruled territories without anyone he knew having made an issue of it. "You can't be so infantile as to think you have to see the world's wonders before you settle down."

Anna reacted in a burst of anguished English, and a flourish that upset her glass of water. "It is not the silly wonders I am after. But what other way can I break out and be *me?*"

"Bravo!"

She looked up with a scowl to find an aging Adonis resplendent in the light blue and scarlet uniform of the Austrian cavalry, his sword gold-knotted at his belt. Under the chandelier, three silver stars winked against his gold-embroidered collar. In a voice that matched his regalia he offered his heartfelt admiration for her spirit.

Nicholas introduced Adonis who said he was enchanted. He was also enchanted to join them and accept a liqueur. Nicholas's polite enquiry about Balkan affairs produced harrowing details in a rich baritone about the mental unbalance of Bosnian youths who, what could you expect, were stuffed with socialism, nationalism, and anarchism. They were being trained to blow up bridges, railways, and officials, all in preparation for an armed struggle that would supposedly liberate the Serbian districts under the Turks and the Hapsburgs, and join them into a supposed Greater Serbia. But, laughed Adonis, he had not sat down to disturb their charming rendezvous, only to pay a warrior's tribute.

"We are so interested," said Anna weakly.

So long as that was the case, said he, Belgrade was a nest of anarchists, and the Chief of Intelligence of the Serbian General Staff had proof they were under the direct influence of the Russian revolutionaries in exile in Lausanne. For that matter he himself had seen a collection of articles of Bosnian authorship with an introduction signed L.T., no less.

"Will His Majesty the Emperor consider some measures to give the subject nationalities more autonomy?" asked Nicholas, never less interested in subject nationalities.

"Some measures perhaps, yes. But if we are realistic we must show we are in command, as the Kaiser showed when he kept his troops on French soil in '71, until reparations were paid up. Discussion with these people will serve no purpose. The Serbians are Orientals, masters at evasion. I must tell you I am profoundly pessimistic about the whole trend," declared Adonis, giving Anna a brilliant smile.

"Which whole trend?" asked Anna.

"Assassination, Miss Hansen. The killer of the Governor of Bosnia, a lunatic who swallowed cyanide then and there on the bridge at Sarajevo, is a Serbian martyr. Do the Serbs condemn him for the murderer he was? Not at all. They are still laying flowers on Zherajitch's grave, such is the situation. The Serbian government itself is behind the secret societies that are plotting to break up the empire."

"So it seems," murmured Nicholas unhelpfully.

"My dear," Adonis addressed him, meaning Mon Cher, "no monarchy is safe while these madmen are loose. They think they are preparing their people as Mazzini did the Italians. Even the imperial army is not what it used to be. It has fallen into the hands of Magyars and Jews—mind you, not from noble and civil service families as in the past. It is seething with typical Levantine intrigue and tactics. Oh yes, we must show we are in command."

Adonis twinkled and shone as he outlined ruthless military measures to deal with obstructionists. Timely small wars prevented big wars. And that reminded him of his next engagement for which he would be late if he did not hurry. He clicked his heels, bowed, and departed with warlike speed and efficiency. The problems of peacemaking descended.

"Compromise is what's needed," said Nicholas, referring to the Balkans, "I think the Emperor would do better with different advisors, don't you?"

They rejected the prescription for little wars. Anna ate some cherries she didn't want. Nicholas drank another cup of coffee. Neither of them mentioned marriage again at lunch though the subject hovered no further away than the headwaiter and could have been summoned with the lift of an eyebrow. They talked about horses. Anna had never watched the Derby and they agreed to go to Epsom the following week. They were in the crowd when a woman ran onto the course and threw herself in front of the King's colt. King George, in shock about his colt, forgot to ask about the woman. She died three days later at Epsom Cottage Hospital without recovering consciousness.

During Nicholas's remaining days in London the Marriot home was convulsed with activity. Nicholas stood in the narrow hall every evening waiting to take Anna out, an aloof and elegant being from a distant, well-organized planet, while women of all shapes and stages of untidiness whirled and eddied around him. On his last evening he found Anna waiting, wan and apologetic that his holiday had not been smooth sailing, and one more tumultuous, moldbreaking thing had chosen to happen during this particular fortnight. There had been so much work to do. She was so sorry that most of her time had been taken up helping with posters and notices and other preparations for Emily Davison's funeral. Nicholas, genuinely aghast at the tragedy, understood, but he could not help asking, with perfect logic he thought, "What has this poor unfortunate woman to do with us?"

It was not a very apt description of a woman who had been to jail eight times, gone on hunger strikes seven times, was force fed forty-nine times, and had twice before attempted martyrdom, Anna informed him as they stood in the hall. This was a woman who hadn't known the meaning of fear or caution. Once she had set fire to a Baptist minister, mistaking him for Lloyd George. Her entire life, except the force feeding, had been of her own making.

And she had been remarkably fortunate. She had done what she set out to do, given her life as a pledge that women would be free. But Nicholas was right. It was nothing to do with "us." We were safe from other people's torments, so safe that liberation stuggles disguised as paint and suicide did not touch a single nerve or chord.

Nicholas touched Anna's cheek with his gloved hand as women streamed out of a room off the hall and started to put on their coats and hats. Portly Mr. Marriot appeared in the busy doorway, his shirtsleeves rolled up, blocking the traffic. His few remaining hairs stood on end. He said "Ah!" distractedly and disappeared again. Little Marriots, on vacation from normal routine, made free with the bannisters.

"You've come to say good-by," said Anna bleakly. "You're leaving for Paris tomorrow."

"I've come to say I'm staying for the funeral," he said.

Anna flung her arms around him with a cry. Mr. Marriot emerged again, said, "My dear Anna, my dear Mr. Wyatt," and guided them to an unoccupied room under the stairs, not much bigger than a cupboard, where every available inch of surface held pyramids of Women's Social and Political Union literature. They squeezed between two pyramids, their arms wrapped around each other.

"I think," Nicholas said carefully, "that we are meant to love and cherish each other very much."

And if that involved cherishing the unknown dead as well, and giving in to year-long journeys to extremely foreign parts, well, it was not what he had had in mind, but so be it. Because he was forced to admit it was loving that mattered most.

He was strangely, powerfully moved by the funeral procession. A tall, yellow-haired girl in a gold dress walked at the head of it, carrying a gold cross. Girls in white holding laurel wreaths and Madonna lilies came behind her. Hundreds in black held irises and peonies. There was a band in scarlet uniforms, and a little group of hunger strikers, released from Holloway, were among the thousands who followed the hearse. Women graduates and doctors marched past in their academic robes in honor of Emily who had graduated with distinction in classics and mathematics from London University, and had taken First Class Honours in English Language and Literature at Oxford. The empty carriage in the procession was Emmeline Pankhurst's. The police had arrested her as she was leaving her flat to attend the funeral, though she had just been released from a three-year sentence of penal servitude for "inciting persons to commit outrages." Nicholas found his own unexpected reaction hard to explain, except that in a land of pageantry it was the first time he had seen it mark an event that signaled the future rather than the past.

In keeping with their new understanding he helped Anna with plans for her trip to India and came back from Paris in September to see her off. He did point out that those who had gone before her had had solid reasons, no shortage of them, from sightseeing and trade to conquest and rule. Among the earliest had been two Chinese monks, three centuries apart, who had braved the incredible journey through Central Asia on foot, to study original Buddhist texts. Hieuen Tsang's walk had taken him six years, and he had spent another eight in India. So was Anna thinking in terms of a fourteen-year absence?

It was proving much harder than Anna had realized to say good-by. She turned from the baskets of geraniums blooming jauntily on Nicholas's balcony, and leaned against him standing close behind her.

"I feel quite widowed," she wept.

"Never speak English when you're all wrought up," he advised, giving her his handkerchief. "You are not widowed because I'm not dead, and in any case we're not even married."

"And now, who knows?" cried Anna, her tears a familiar sign of obstinancy, not weakness, so Nicholas left her with the geraniums and busied himself with the telephone and telegraph, arranging for her to be met and taken care of at stages of her voyage. As a man who knows a rare investment when he sees one, he had no intention of letting her pull a Hieuen Tsang on him.

Henry instructed his bearer to give Miss Hansen her post before she left. As she might be coming every day, she could take Sir Nitin's letters too. He would have them brought here from the post office. And she was to be given lunch if she came at lunchtime.

"Coming after lunch," said the bearer.

"Then give her tea."

"Going before tea."

"Well then look after her. Water. Fruit. Whatever she wants."

The bearer put Henry's lunch tray down on his desk and retired to the corridor where an office peon who only carried files held court to those who fetched and carried heavier things. The gardener and his underlings were smoking and chatting near the morning-glories with the cook and his underling. A coolie who had trudged miles with a load of firewood strapped to his back, and supported by a band around his forehead, delivered it and left. The sweeper was somewhere around within call for most of the day with a toilet-cleaning job no one else would do, though underlings could be ordered to do most other jobs and during a natural disaster or a national emergency the peon might carry a saucepan and the cook a postage stamp. And all these people had wives and numerous children. One saw dismally few of those whom one governed and one was careful not to touch the honeycomb's whorls and intricacies. Interference was the hallmark of the vulgar conqueror, here today and gone tomorrow. Empire builders had profits to make, apart from other more exalted reasons for keeping the peace. Angry hornets played havoc with Scottish business and with growing markets for the City and Westminster. A stir in the corridor told Henry that Anna had arrived. He ate his lunch, read a newspaper, and got up to take a turn around the garden before his afternoon appointments began.

Problems quite often did not end, but they had a definite beginning. He could date his and Stella's from Khudiram's execution. She had insisted on attending it. It was so soon after her confinement, he had used Jennie's birth instead of political unrest as an excuse to beg her to stay at home.

"When you've been through what I have, Henry, you can face anything. I'd go to this hanging if I were on my deathbed. It's the least I can do. This is the animal who killed Mrs. Kennedy and her daughter. It might have been me, or any of us."

She had done her father credit, sitting stoically through the ordeal, impervious to the crowd of hundreds who had collected to cheer the condemned man. Henry's ritual duty-bound presence made less of an impression than Stella's, and his anxiety for her safety helped him to keep a grip on his own composure. When the thin young body was jerked from the ground, a current of boiling emotion surged through the crowd. Cries of "Vande Mataram" were lost in a tumult of shouting and wailing. Every instinct warned Henry that order hung by a strand. Yet in the terrible uncertainty of the public's raw reaction, his only real fear was that he might be the stranger Stella needed protection from. He had stood sweating in his appointed place, a symbol of authority, questioning the authority he was exercising, while his official mind worked rapidly on cordoning and containing the crowd. But the confusion died away, and people started to leave.

He saw Stella to her carriage and went to his office, telling himself it was natural enough to feel a shaken revulsion. One needed a second skin to get through normal official routine, which today had included a hanging. What he doubted was his ability to grow one. It made him unfit for the job he had, and, much moreso, for Stella, who in living through Jennie's wracking birth had been reborn herself, mysteriously strong and able. When Pryor came to Bihar on official business with his wife, Stella made a lasting impression on the two of them. It was harder for Henry to go his heretical way after that, with a triple alliance believing so firmly in him. The Pryors had simple, comforting solutions. Given time, and the right wife—and Henry had both—nothing could go very wrong. He had risen fast. He couldn't spoil his chances now. He was destined for better things once he had put his flawed reasoning behind him. Unfortunately the flawed reasoning had been committed to paper. Henry had written cautious screeds recommending policy changes, suggesting everyone was not an assassin and whole populations could not be treated with suspicion. He had implied the heart of the matter was an equal relationship, and it would only come of mixing. With those sentiments, Pryor told him, it was not going to be easy convincing the top brass that Henry was sound. But the case for his removal from the turbulence of Bihar was obvious, and Pryor was now one of the top brass himself. He, personally, would do all he could to have Henry transferred as soon as there was a vacancy in his own state. Some peace and quiet would work wonders. Pryor said he could guarantee there'd be more of it now with Tilak out of the way. They had come to dinner on their last night. It was stifling indoors and they were dining on the verandah.

Henry, who had read the article in *Kesari* for which Tilak was prosecuted, remarked, "Frankly it didn't sound seditious to me."

"It's not always easy to judge sedition. The judge has to make up his mind what effect a piece of writing is going to have on general readers."

"A friend of mine sent me Mr. Keir Hardie's article in the *Labour Leader*. He compares Tilak's reputation in literature with Chaikovsky's, the writer who's in jail without trial in Russia, or with our own Alfred Russel Wallace in a science."

"Never heard of the publication," said Pryor, "and Hardie's a crank. Pacifist, socialist. His mother was a servant. Hardly a recommendation. The *Times* has upheld the judgment."

An overpowering scent of night-blooming jasmine came to them on the hot, heavy air. Stella complained it gave her a headache.

"Sitting near it is like getting too much sun. I ought to get the bush dug up and planted further away from the house."

"Don't go in for any big changes now," Mary Pryor advised. "Robert is going to see to it you're out of here as soon as possible. I don't know how you've stood the strain as long as you have."

But the transfer had taken unexpectedly long. Stella had finished breast feeding. She was recovering her austere ballerina beauty. And Henry had had time to dream of an alternative career. Specifically, politics.

"I had no idea you were getting so restless, Henry."

Less restless than the world around him, he pointed out, if you looked at the Russo-Japanese War as just one example of established theories being turned inside out, and the white race getting thrashed by yellow men.

"But do you know *anyone* in either the Liberal or Conservative party who could be the least possible help?" she worried.

"I wasn't thinking of them. There's a third party now with twenty-nine members in Parliament."

"Miners," said Stella.

"They're not all miners."

Stella sat quietly appalled, as deadly calm as she had been at the execution. But suddenly it was too much for her. She turned to him in outright desperate appeal, afire with her own intensity.

"Don't do it, Henry. Let's hang on. If you'll only hang on a little longer, I *know*, I just *know* everything's going to be all right."

Another woman, bereft of argument, would have sulked or pleaded for her own sake. But Stella's appeal was to faith and their shared, shining future. It was so unlike the Pryors' bland "All will be well," so far from the temperate zone the Pryors of the world inhabited that it made a clean sweep of Henry's doubts. The doubts came back later but he had made his choice, and his choice had been Stella, not historical reasons and forces. He had not resigned from the Indian Civil Service because of the unearthly radiance in his wife's face one evening. It was as simple as that. Too simple evidently. He had had to invent more complicated answers to satisfy those who had counted on his entry into the party.

Stella and Jennie spent the next hot season with Mary

Pryor in Naini Tal. When Henry was transferred and they left Bihar, they stopped with the Pryors in Lucknow on their way to Himapur. By then Jennie was their joint treasure, and they laughed at her antics as she staggered around the Pryors' garden under their combined watchful gaze. Like any reunited family of five, they had a lot to laugh about.

"At least we'll be in good weather," said Stella, anticipating Himapur, "marvelous for Henry and Jennie."

"Your guardian angel doesn't seem very concerned about herself," Pryor remarked, he and Mary hardly able to take their indulgent, admiring eyes off Stella.

She looked cool, crisp, and heartbreakingly disciplined in white. Only the red hibiscus Henry had put in her hair was wilting in the heat.

The bedroom door was open. It was Anna's idea of Stella's room, ivory walls, bedspreads inset with lace, frilled and looped curtains, a washstand with a white enamel jug and basin, watercolors of spring and summer gardens in oval frames. The nursery next door was locked. Jennie had gone home for good. The library was across the hall. Its comfortable shabby chairs, wool rugs, and packed bookshelves had no particular stamp of gender. Stella must have left it as she found it, but the gardener kept it filled with flowers. A long window opened onto tubs of hydrangea and clean pebbly gravel. In here was the vibrating silence of well-used rooms. If one sat here long enough it would magnify into a crickets' orchestra. Curious to think of a man sitting here alone hour after hour when his work was done. It was generally women who stayed home and grew old waiting, men who came and went, no questions asked. From her deep chair Anna heard Henry Brewster giving instructions. She went to the window and watched him walk across the

wide emerald lawn to the conifers at the edge of the garden. There, in defiance of the laws of art and nature, a
human figure of stature and surprising significance stood
braced below an immense irregular snowline. Perhaps
because one could not see his drawn and tired face at that
distance. Sir Basu had told her malaria affected the liver
and was a very debilitating illness. His next home leave
would put him right. But Anna found it hard to believe his
illness was confined to malaria or that home leaves cured
grieving souls.

"There is no need to jump to conclusions," Sir Basu had
said. "How do you know Mrs. Brewster has gone for good?
Has he told you so?"

"No, but nine months is a long time to be away."

"Not at all. People have gone away for years at a time
and come back."

"Men," said Anna, "to Crusades and other adventures.
And indentured labor."

"Possibly," he conceded grudgingly, though he had the
gravest doubts about her historical sense, and her statistics
were likely to be as extraordinary. "Marriage is not the
Crusades, Miss Hansen. I have known cases of wives who
left their husbands to come back after a suitable period of
separation, when tempers cooled. Partings work wonders."

Neither of them being authorities on marriage, they had
left it at that.

One of the books Anna had taken off its shelf was a
translation of a Muslim lady's love letters, signed "Your
fainting invalid," to her heartless, gallivanting East India
Company lover. What else had there been to do but faint
on couches (for those who had couches, and time to faint)?
No adventuring. No astronomy or physics. No stocks and
shares to play with. Never even a hangover or a black eye
in a brawl. Not much of anything but four walls and lam-

entations. The Portuguese nun deserted by her French chevalier had spent the rest of her days clawing at the walls of her Franciscan convent. Madame Butterfly had died of song. Penelope had passed her nights unraveling the tapestry she wove by day. And the one or two who had run away had come to a sticky end, in suicide or disgrace. But Stella, instead of falling about in a faint, had had the guts to pack up and leave and make a life somewhere else, though she, too, might as well have been the figment of someone's literary imagination. There was nothing to prove a flesh and blood woman had ever been here, except two clashing photographs of her and a white bedroom, sterile as a gauze bandage.

The men who had appointments with the Collector as they called him, used an entrance near his office. Their voices sounded far away as they left the building. Footsteps in the corridor, canvas shoes on the gravel outside, belonged to the household and were pleasant reminders that people were about, the day's activities proceeding. Otherwise they barely grazed her consciousness. She had seldom felt so peaceful. Copenhagen, London, Madras, and Calcutta were not particularly peaceful places, but this was not a matter of place. And it wasn't entirely a question of peace. For some reason she was quite content not to understand, she felt an involvement. It was unexpected, and troublesome. It had arrived at the wrong time, at the tail end of her travels, when it was almost time to start thinking about her return. Henry Brewster was an enigmatic personality, which gave an unusual twist to his domestic crisis. The smoke here had to be made from some wonderfully interesting fire. She wrote him a note, listing the two books she was borrowing, and left it under the glass paperweight on his desk in the library. At the front door she

met the bearer waiting for her with the gardener's underling, who, he said, was going to walk behind her carrying
her letters. She could give him the books. Anna floundered
between argument and pantomime, gave up, and handed
her books to the underling, who nodded and smiled, quite
mystified by the delay.

She walked back, thoughtful about Henry Brewster's
domestic crisis. It had gone on so long, he should have been
adjusted to it by now. Marlowe Croft, her other neighbor,
would probably sail through a crisis and come out fighting
fit. She was sure crises rolled off him like water off a duck's
back. Croft had religion. But it was Brewster who made her
think of candles, incense, altars, and the brooding vaults
of great cathedrals. Croft had the true believer's tough
workaday religion, which had about as much glamour and
mystique to it as *Das Kapital.* Only a skeptic could be struck
by religious lightning and be transformed in a blinding
instant. Great personal grief might do it. There were so
many roads to Damascus, and the lightning fell according
to its own rules. She and Nicholas were not the sort to see
visions, and Sir Basu's scientific genius ruled him out as a
candidate for revelation. But Brewster could be one of the
elect, earmarked for mystical experience and another
dimension of life. If she were wrong and the love of God
didn't claim him, he would still be heard of as a unique
administrator, a celebrated traitor to his own cause. Personal happiness, or the pursuit of it, didn't have much to
do with such lives.

Lulu, the ways of the plantation will not work here,"
Marlowe laid down a golden rule at breakfast. "We're
after their souls, not profit, and we can't bludgeon
them into believing in God. It took Moses forty years to
reach the Promised Land. He had to change his people's
hearts and purify himself first."

New Zealand butter was melting deliciously and by
sheerest chance into Lulu's toast because Stella Brewster
had done the disappearing trick. Nothing had ever been
sent over in her time, but butter and condensed milk and
Triptree's strawberry jam with whole strawberries in it
probably reminded the D.M. of his disappeared wife, though
Marlowe called it generosity. Why shouldn't Moses take
forty years to reach the Promised Land when the average
age was two hundred? Sarah could have a baby at ninety
and Methuselah's mum could put nine hundred candles on
his cake. Jacob hadn't cared if he waited seven years to
marry a woman and then married the wrong one. Never
mind, better luck next time, but Marlowe didn't have that
much time. And his high ideals, which made him the great
man he was, gave her frightening passing thoughts of him,
stooped, white-haired, churchless, delivering the Word of
God in a quavering voice from a pulpit surrounded by a
thousand miles of sand dunes, malarial swamp, or virgin

jungle with not a pygmy or a camel in sight. It was the terrible price he would pay for his greatness. The quaver in his ancient future voice haunted her long after the thought passed.

She had gone into a trance listening to his last sermon in a little country church close to her father's estate before his trial and jail term. What would Jesus say, yes, what would Jesus say? What if He took a walk among the miserable and downtrodden on the neighboring plantation? What if He stood face to face with the Viceroy in Calcutta as He'd stood face to face with Pontius Pilate? What if He took a whirlwind tour of the slums in Calcutta, capital of the empire, as he had through the temple of Jerusalem? Lulu hadn't bothered about the answers. It was the magnetic power of his voice that had made the routine of rising to her feet and singing "Onward Christian Soldiers" acts of palpitating surrender. She had tasted the salt of her tears as her own tremulous voice sang. At home her father threw tantrums.

"Put you in a trance, has he? Well, it's nothing to the trance you'll be in with the thrashing you'll get from me if you don't snap out of it, my girl."

Daddy wouldn't have laid a finger on her, she was his little pet. But the point was, he couldn't have laid a finger on her. He didn't have it in him any more. There was a curse on indigo. The trade had been drying up for years. Other planters had switched to tea and coffee. But Daddy refused to because of Marlowe. They had become the same red flag to him, and he went around with his head lowered, ready to charge.

"Cock of the walk, is he? He won't be much longer," he would shout to no one in particular at dinner. "No bloody chamber of commerce is telling me what to plant." Then suddenly, disturbingly discovering the two women at the dining table, and lumping them together, "What church is this you sneaked off to? You've got a church of your own, haven't you? What were you doing when she sneaked off, hiding under Percy bloody Shelley and the bird that never shit?"

Lulu didn't dare tell him she had joined an upstart church she didn't know the name of and fallen under the spell of the enemy. She was afraid of what he would work himself up to, and how he would punish the furniture, the servants, and her mother, apart from herself. He hadn't been himself since Marlowe and indigo had joined forces to jerk the ground from under his feet. And now she was afraid Marlowe's greatness hadn't been the same since having to scale itself down to Himapur size. There were so few people to talk to, let alone preach to, that the bounce in one's voice petered out like a tennis ball served smashingly on a hard court when there was no one on the other side of the net. Telling Marlowe so was as pointless as it had been trying to convince her father that indigo was dead and gone. But she was determined to be a loyal wife. She helped herself to strawberry jam and stopped criticizing.

"Do you think our job is easier?" continued Marlowe. "We will never get it done unless we recapture the spirit of the catacombs. But we have to go carefully. You know this is my last chance."

Lulu's heart danced. Personally she would be overjoyed if they were given their marching orders. She longed to get out and go somewhere else, anywhere else, most of all home, but she didn't like to imagine, not for a second, what being ordered out of India and having to make a fresh start in some other back-of-beyond would do to Marlowe. Churches like Marlowe's only went to backs-of-beyond. There wasn't a ghost of a chance of going home, either his or hers, and home would kill Marlowe. She thought of the prophets, Elijah, and Isaiah, and the other great speechmakers, and what a nice suburban life and tea-party routine would have done to them. Taken the wind out of their sails, it would have.

"We're here to make friends and win people's confidence," Marlowe told her. "It takes a while to get established and become part of the community. Remember we've got a church to build."

A spark of pure wrath churned Lulu's insides.

"Who exactly am I supposed to make friends *with?* I did my best with Stella Brewster, but she's too grand for the likes of us. And I'm tired of hearing about the church from morning till night. The way you go on, one would think you're planning to build the Canterbury Cathedral instead of a little old wooden shack, where you'll have no one but coolies and servants for a congregation."

"Be careful, Lulu." Three words more subduing than a mouthful of profanity from her father. At such times pieces of ice touched the top of her spine, and she could feel once again the thrill and throb of his soaring belief in every vein.

"The church will be built, and no mistake," he warned. "I've staked my life, my very soul on it. In time, this will be a Christian land. It took centuries to Christianize the Scandinavians, though they were Europeans like us. I'll do it here. I'll make something out of nothing. I intend to get started as soon as the District Magistrate hands down his decision."

"I wouldn't count on him handing down any decision," said Lulu, lapsing into Marlowe's speech. "He's in no hurry."

"What makes you think so?" asked Marlowe, all attention.

Greatness didn't always mean common sense, so she explained how it was with district magistrates, the hemming-and-hawing and excuses even when they wanted to be helpful, which this one didn't.

"I don't know how you've come to that conclusion. He has been very courteous and understanding. He's being as helpful as he can."

"Anyway he looks a wreck," said Lulu, giving up. "He ought to be glad her ladyship left him, instead of moping as if he'd lost an arm and a leg. Good riddance is what I say. She must have been up to something."

"Well, it's none of our business. And we can't take sides between man and wife. How do we know who was at fault?"

"But we *do* know she went off bag and baggage," said Lulu placidly, "even her dog. Why would she have taken the dog if she meant to come back? No one would want to cart a dog around all those bends in the road just to cart it back again."

Marlowe thought it over. "You may be right, Lulu. If she's not coming back, it will be a bitter blow to her husband and it could do his career a lot of harm. I suppose he could give it up and go home, but if I'm any judge of character, he wouldn't do that any more than I would pack up and go home if I had a setback. He will stay right here and do his duty."

Marlowe finished his breakfast and made straight for the woodshed in the garden where he was giving a carpenter measurements for benches that would make a room in their house look more like a classroom. Lulu strolled out onto the veranda to finish her toast. The air was soft and damp and had a nip to it, but the morning mist was clearing. Sunlight sieved through treetops to lie gently along the slope rising from the road to their house. Sixteen little black children (brown, Lulu, brown, and what bleeding difference did that make) would soon be straggling up the slope, and presently Tantanna Hansen, or whatever fool name she liked every Tom, Dick, and Harry to call her, would be along it with her whitish hair in a plait down her back, to take the exercise class. She insisted on starting the day with it because the early morning air was supposed to be better to breathe. More like it, she had to get back to her notes on Sir Whatnot's howling vegetables.

Half an hour later Lulu was back on the veranda with her last cup of tea to watch T. H. leading the little blacks in exercise. She knew T. H. had arrived because they started hollering Tantannas, delirious as Hosannas. Lulu called out "Yoo-hoo Marlowe" to Marlowe who had come out of the woodshed to watch, his set and fixed face relaxing at the sight, but he didn't hear her. She knew he didn't see T. H. either. He saw his shack of a church materializing before his eyes and all the dreams of his mission being realized in shrieks of "Tantanna" as the children chased each other round and round her. It was plainly the best part of their day. She clapped her hands, the bedlam stopped and they darted into a crooked, lively line, short and tall ones all muddled instead of in order of their heights. The sweeper's scarecrow child hung back, kicking stones with his bare toes. Marlowe propelled him, wriggling and squirming, into the line, but he was out of it and back to stone kicking before Marlowe's back was turned. Coaxed forward again, he ground to a halt several yards from the other children, a wound-up toy whose mechanism had expired. But Marlowe was cheerfully winding him up again. Lulu's breath came faster. Taboos as feared as the God of Abraham rose spectrally between Marlowe's magnetism and the jerking, twitching toy. She managed to shout, "Marlowe!" just as the class began, and he walked off to the woodshed.

T. H. raised her bare arms slowly sideways, palms up, to

the sky, lifting her face to the sun. The hooligans copied her clumsily. Instead of getting the woman to come to church services, Marlowe had let her foist all this sun gazing on them and he was as pleased as punch about it. If he hadn't been in such a tizzy about his church he would hardly call this exercise. Lulu twirled the remains of her tea around in her cup and flicked it into a flowerpot. She remembered the commands chirped out by the games mistress at her school. Up! Down! In! Out! Shoulders back! Forward march! And so forth. This regimen, faces lifted to the sun, was no more exercise than dogs got when they bayed at the moon. They should have been learning gymnastics. There wasn't enough real activity in the entire half hour to tire a cockroach, let alone a child. And there was certainly no reason to have them flat on their backs on the grass "relaxing" at the end of it, with some of them actually dozing off instead of looking sharp about lessons. No wonder they were having the time of their lives. When T. H. clapped her hands and cried "So!" they jumped up like jack-in-the-boxes and started racing around like maniacs again instead of quieting down for Christian Endeavor. Only the sweeper's wisp of a brat backed off and sat down vacant-eyed under a tree.

Marlowe, hearing the commotion, crossed over from the woodshed and Lulu saw T. H. waving her arms in the air explaining to him above the racket that Surya Namaskar, or Salute to the Sun, was part of the ancient system of yoga, unfortunately not practiced in the West. Marlowe was looking jolly and kind. Lulu rang a brisk bell and the children, all but the sweeper's brat, followed her indoors. He trailed in when the others were seated and sat down warily at the back of the room, in the opposite corner from the drinking goblet, leaving plenty of space on the floor between him and his classmates. Before she could begin Marlowe came in and urged the boy to move up. The boy blinked. Nothing else about him moved.

"Okay, we'll let it go this time," he told Lulu, "but we've got to move him up to sit with the rest of them. A kid's scared of a bicycle, put him on a bicycle and give it a shove. I was so scared of water, I wouldn't learn to swim. One day my father threw me in. Nobody ever learned to swim so fast."

This time the moment did not pass. Lulu was glued to it and it had nothing to do with a decrepit Marlowe and a quavering voice. The pitfalls of his greatness were already upon them. Marlowe had insane ideas about changing the world, starting with any few square feet he happened to be standing on. First it had been indigo plantations, now he was making something out of nothing in Himapur. Someone would really have to tell him that admitting an untouchable to a class with shopkeepers' and other high-caste children was not the same as putting him on a bicycle and giving it a shove. The pure in heart like Marlowe couldn't be expected to think of these things. She told him.

"You never should've made him join," she finished. "Besides he's much younger than the others and he doesn't know a word of English."

But Marlowe insisted with the tremendous dignity she admired so much, "No one under this roof is an untouchable. I want you to put that undemocratic idea right out of your mind, Lulu."

He persuaded the brat to move up an inch or two. As soon as he left, taking the spirit of the catacombs with him, the class settled down. The brat shifted back, the last row moved forward, and Lulu got on with Christian Endeavor.

. . .

Anna started the letter in her mind on her way home. The only thing she had in common with Paul the Apostle was that she wrote to Nicholas as Paul was supposed to have prayed, without ceasing, and like Paul's prayers, most of her letters remained in her head. Silent communion was in the nature of lasting relationships. Absence should make no difference to them. Unhappily it did. Silent communion with another mortal had its definite drawbacks. Nicholas attended gala events in Paris and London and his last letter said he had been invited by the Queen of Rumania to her summer castle at Sinaia. He was the world's most eligible escort since the beginning of time. Generations of European and British aristocrats had brought up their daughters to be the perfect wives of men like Nicholas, and there had been time enough for an entire cold buffet of hands to be laid out, waiting to be asked for, while Anna recorded the neurotic tendencies of celery. The woman he had married and lost in a hunting accident three years ago had shone even in the ranks of the perfect. From all he had said about her, Anna had reason to believe their relationship had been a sonnet of sorts. By now, with the six thousand miles Anna had put between herself and Nicholas, he might have embarked on a ballad or a narrative poem with some other woman. The field of the cloth of gold spread out for his enjoyment was outrageous, unequal and unfair. St. Paul's communion with the Almighty had never been threatened by the inner furies Anna's mental correspondence had to cope with. But the result was that when she got down to pen and paper, her actual letters practically wrote themselves. She had nothing in common, years later, with popular songs begging "you-hoo" to "luh-huv" "me-hee," the language of retarded apes, if apes had been learning some moronic form of basic English, with its boohoo-hooing about "luh-huv-huv."

Dearest Nicholas, she wrote with a fine-pointed pen in the slanted script of her actual letter that afternoon, the Bengali community of Himapur—why not the whole of Himapur, I ask, when he is so famous—want to make a reception for Sir Basu. Usually he says no to invitations because they interrupt him when he has come here to be alone, but as these are Bengalis, how can he refuse? He says it would not be gracious to his own community. I have taught the cook to prepare Danish apple cake but Sir Basu says the Bengali community is going to make the whole arrangement. I am invited. This means I must leave half an hour before him as I can not see myself carried by coolies. I will try to find out if there is a shortcut to the house of Mr. and Mrs. Banerji, the hosts. It is not far if a crow could fly straight through the hill. Up via the mall makes it long. I can not persuade Sir Basu to walk. Once was enough, to the District Magistrate's which is close to us. With me walking the question arises of clothes. I would like to go (how I would!) looking like an illustration out of *Chic Parisien*, but that is impossible without a rickshaw. In the most stylish skirt I brought with me I have to hobble. I am glad to hear styles are changing and one can take a step forward without falling flat on one's face. But it would be best of all if designers would discover that women have two legs just like men. That is enough English for this time. (It is time you learned Danish.)

She continued in French: Henry Brewster, whom I described earlier, is a mold-breaking man, but as the imperial mold is not likely to break, I should call him a mold-cracker instead. Quite some cracks he has made, mainly by being informal and friendly. He has a sympathetic way with him, strides about the town and the hills without a scrap of self-importance. I had always thought of a colonial officer as being full of his own prestige. Brewster is an eye-

opener besides being a mold-cracker. I get the feeling his
wife doesn't have his easy manner. You would know what
I mean if you could see the local photographer's grand official portrait of her. As you know, pictures are evidence as
much as other forms of evidence. If that's how Madhav
Rao sees her, many others must too. I hope I shall still be
here when she returns. The talk is she won't. After all she
has been away nine months. But on the other hand wives
don't generally leave husbands, so I don't know what to
make of it. Brewster is too proud a man to feel sorry for,
but I long for her to return to put him out of his misery.
He is quite nakedly suffering and it is hard to watch him
and remain unmoved. It is odd that he looks like the priest,
and the beefy missionary, Croft, like an empire builder.

Anna finished her letter and took it to the post office
herself. The postmaster, a local man, informed her there
was a convenient shorter route to the Banerji house, which
the mail runner sometimes used, if she did not mind going
along the dark side of the hill, so called because the sun
scarcely penetrated the dense woods. He would not recommend it himself. No, not to do with safety. There was
little crime to worry about in these parts, nothing that a
junior police officer could not handle, but who likes to walk
through dark places alone? Going home that way to try it
out Anna realized she was somewhere below the rock where
her fall had landed her. The path that led to the clearing
where she had come across Brewster and Croft must be
straight up the hill. It was a hillside with endless vertical
possibilities. And the little postmaster had been wrong. At
this hour sunlight filtered through the silent pines. Wild
white rose creeper curled around deodar branches and hung
down from them. Clumps of black-eyed Susans and berry
bushes gave their surroundings a friendly charm. Summer

picnickers and pony riders had come here even if the local people avoided it. A few days later, on her way to the Banerjis, she filled a basket with wild raspberries to take along.

The Banerjis' drawing room had a bow window overlooking the garden. A man sat on the cushioned window seat. Anna had an impression of sparkling gaiety and humor flowing in a stream of mellifluous language to the semicircle of adorers at his feet. It gave her a shock to discover it was Sir Basu. His graceful pleated *dhoti,* the immemorial elegance of the white silk shawl over one shoulder, the rich amusement he radiated, reminded her of Roman senators off their pedestals, spinning Latin yarns with friends and Romans. Behind him the top of a row of hollyhocks made a trim, erect contrast to the silk saris and fluid vowel sounds in the room. An archway separated the room from a dining alcove. Anna saw the corner of a white tablecloth falling in folds to the carpet and two servants putting dishes down on it. She stood stricken at the entrance with the basket of berries over her arm. She had discovered on the way here that the berries had no taste. She had got on a ship and arrived like a mailbag. Then she had picked berries hard as bullets for a banquet. And for the first time she marveled at Didi hiring her, an apparition out of nowhere.

"How nice of you to come, Miss Hansen," Mrs. Banerji took musical charge of her and the basket. "We have been so curious to meet you. Fancy Didi! Nitin-da has been telling us it was Didi who found you. Nitin-da said he had no idea!"

They were joined by other professional vocalists, or talented amateurs to judge by the loving lilt of their English, and every one of them was calling Sir Basu elder brother, grandfather, or uncle, though Anna knew he had no blood relations in Himapur. It was apparently their custom to be related, blood or not. It made her feel stark, solitary, and sudden. Henry Brewster had officialdom, Croft had his mission, and Mrs. Croft had Croft. But all history's travelers had been men. The most accomplished, Marco Polo, had had the sense to melt into the scene and become indistinguishable from it, while she, Anna, had had the audacity to serve fricadella. She heard her hostess, a nonstop chatterbox, invite her to help herself to creations of sugar, butter, and cream.

"How thin you are, Miss Hansen. Please eat. Above all, Didi! She's so hopelessly old-fashioned. How did she ever find you? She never leaves her house. Do you call that a helping?"

Anna, not required to answer, ate. The other women chimed in about Didi's hopeless backwardness, running out of breath and leaving their sentences fascinatingly suspended for each other to fill in. They were all dipping into a communal conversation, jointly owned, instead of taking turns at it. Anna dipped in once or twice experimentally herself and then, confidently, more often. No one fired questions at her. Nor had Didi. Not one solid fact or date had been mentioned in the course of their meeting, or another shorter one when Anna had gone to say good-by. And if Didi had made enquiries to satisfy herself about Anna's credentials, it couldn't have got her very far. Anna had been as sprung out of nowhere in Caluctta as she was here. Quite a change from job application in earnest. Your qualifications Miss Hansen? None? Previous experience? None at all? Family background? Not *the* Johannes Hansen? The very one? A pause. Then, I see. Well you will appreciate our difficulty. Parents, you know, have to be particularly careful about the upbringing of their impressionable young daughters and the influences tender young minds come into contact with. Job hunting had barged into one dead end after another until her father had written a fuming letter to the Marriots about the decline of the West and they had taken her to their feminist bosom.

"How boring you must find it here, no shops, nothing," said Mrs. Banerji. "If Mrs. Brewster had been here you would have someone to mix with and you've eaten nothing, I've been watching your plate. Nilima, bring another *luddoo* for Miss Hansen. But I'm glad she's away for her sake. Last rainy season the poor thing told me the rain drumming on the roof would be the end of her."

Everyone agreed Mrs. Brewster had hated the rain.

Nilima, who had brought the *luddoo* said, "Nitin-da has tried and tried to persuade the D.M. to start a European club, and an Indian club, but Mr. Brewster doesn't like the idea. You know he he feels."

"How does *she* feel?" asked Anna.

"Who? Oh, you mean Mrs. Brewster? About a club?"

No one had asked her, or she hadn't spoken. Whichever it was, the view of Mrs. Brewster on a community matter was a blank, although her reaction to the rain drumming maddeningly on the roof was widely known.

The Banerjis' male guests, bound by legal and academic training, had got into the habit of completing their sentences and weighing their words, though maybe they got liberated when they retired. Anna heard one of them remark, "Loneliness is the lot of men who are ahead of their times." Another said, "I may say there is nothing small-minded about the District Magistrate." There was emphatic agreement with both statements.

"Would you say that is true of Mrs. Brewster?" asked Anna.

Plans for Departure

"I really couldn't tell you," said the man earnestly. "It is hard to tell about ladies. And one does not know the wife of a high official."

But of course one did know the views and tastes of the mighty when the mighty wanted them known. On the way home Anna remembered the story Didi had told her of the delightful Lady B., a governor's wife whose delicate hints to rajas and maharajas had left gaping holes in their jewelry vaults. The word had got around in the network and minor eleven-gun-salute maharajas who had less to part with had panicked and taken to burying their treasure and forgetting where it was in the hope that sons and grandsons, and other irregular but well-loved offspring, would dig and find it one day. But naturally the princely alliance with the Crown meant everything couldn't be buried. The odd handful of priceless pearls or string of rubies ended up gift-wrapped on the departing train. Just before leaving India the Governor and his delightful wife had paid a farewell visit to the twenty-one-gun-salute Maharaja of Jainagar who traced his ancestry to the moon goddess and who wore emeralds the size of breakfast eggs when he romped with his favorite children by his Number Two Maharani. He must have been romping with the little dears when the delicate hint was delivered in advance of the Governor's party, and had been too engrossed playing "Button, button, who's got the button" to send a reply. In any case, Their Excellencies arrived the very next day. Between the tiger shoot and the polo match Her poor Excellency had had to poke His Highness playfully and ask for the teeniest weeniest hint of what he was going to give her as a parting present because the suspense was becoming unbearable. "Surprise, surprise, Your Excellency!" H. H. had crooned, wagging a playful forefinger back at her and the court artist had made a charming

informal sketch of them like that. Suspense had mounted through the parade but with military traditions to be upheld by both sides there was naturally no playful poking and wagging. At the ball that evening, "We're off the day after, your Highness, can't you just—?" Lady B. had soundlessly mouthed the words during thunderous applause between dances as the court juggler stood on his head balancing a garden with lakes, fountains, and little pear trees on a double-decker solid gold platform across his feet featuring the state's flora and fauna in all their breathtaking variety, hand wrought in miniature masterpieces of jewelcraft. H. H., lip reading the message, had immediately mouthed "Surprise!" in return. They sat shoulder to shoulder at the final banquet, His Highness displaying a chestful of fabled ancestral diamond necklaces, though of course the delicate hint had been about his egg-sized emeralds. He had responded to the swooning light in Her Excellency's eyes with "Till the train, till the train!" and to her rapture had tapped out a smart little tattoo of the refrain with his dessert spoon on her fish fork just before the fish course came. Their eyes exchanged signals of perfect understanding once again as the table rose to toast the King. Next day, the gleaming train, the vermilion carpet, the anthem, the pomp, the show, the speech, and as the Governor's train rolled, H. H. the Maharaja of Jainagar thrust a magnificently decorated casket containing a hundred or so karats at least in through the window into the A.D.C.'s arms and out popped a poodle. "Surpri-i-i-se!" chanted H. H. as the train sped away.

None of which made Stella Brewster's presence or absence easier to understand.

As his interest in career, advancement and the affairs of the great world dwindled, the world-in-miniature he dealt with moved closer, like the mountains every evening. He took nothing for granted in it, not even the chair he sat on. Here, mystery was a house with chairs, the bungalow of the being known as Klekter. The ultimate mystery was the Collector himself. Who else would ask, "How old are you?" in the courthouse at the end of the mall and be dissatisfied with the straightforward reply: "Twenty, twenty-one, twenty-two," with good-natured hill accents from the back of the room adding "He has not completed twenty-four, he is speaking the truth." Who would go on insisting, "What time was it when you arrived with your goat at the meat market that morning?" and show impatience when told it was afternoon, not morning, so it must have been twelve-one-two? Oho, Klekter, why this anxiety about time and age, so long as it is certain it was earlier or later than some other event? Time has a meaning, and it is day coming after night, wrinkles after youth, and toothlessness after teeth. A ticking machine has other uses. Borrowed from a shopkeeper or a city-returned hillman, it can be held up to a tearful infant's ear to make him break into a bewildered smile. They gave Klekter and whichever witness happened to be on the stand,

emancipating advice and alternatives. The bogus Blavatsky's theories would sound more intelligent in the courthouse than What time was it when? No one would turn a
hair if Klekter announced he had seen an astral body floating in suspended animation between death and rebirth. He
wished he had. It would at least put him down firmly in
one camp, either the Himapur honeycomb, or Pryorland.
With no place to call home he felt like an astral body himself, still floating when the court closed and the audience
trekked back to smoky warrens shared with a jumble of
sheep and goats. No imperial glory, Britain's or earlier, had
penetrated the warrens. It made him wonder about other
golden ages of progress and renaissance.

Pryor's visit, less than a year ago, had gone badly. He had
got down to business immediately on arrival without
allowing time to get used to the altitude. Pink with exertion and out of breath, he had made a quick survey of
industrial possibilities and asked Henry to follow through.
But in spite of Pryor's energy on foot and horseback during
working hours, Henry's most vivid recollection was of a
short, tidy man in evening dress, sitting with his fingertips
steepled on top of his tummy after dinner, his little legs
stretched peacefully toward the grate, the fire glancing off
his rosy cheeks, and the high shine of his city shoes. He
and Stella had a leisurely gossip about the Willy's-Knight
he had ordered from England and the new Governor's food
fads while Henry debated whether Pryor's bedroom slippers had pom-poms on them. By a sleight-of-tongue, conversation during coffee had wiped out dinnertime. It seemed
on eon ago that Stella had sat between them, white with
self-control, interrupting Henry's side of the argument with
occasional sharp comments. After a while it had not mattered. When dinner ended, Henry knew there were argu-

ments words could not answer. In the firelight his thoughts
turned to pompoms, Wee Willie Winkie nightcaps, and what
Pryor had been like as a tot.

The past months had tested his endurance but all things
considered, Henry felt fairly normal during office hours.
Office time, contained by office space, sealed off by curtains, carpet, and filing cabinets, was well within his management and control. The rest of time stretched awe-
inspiringly for miles in all directions. Books he was reading got finished one after another in rapid, meaningless
succession. He couldn't remember exactly what he had done
yesterday but years away a cart creaked up the road, its
bells signaling ice cream. As he lay in bed his childhood
sea writhed tiredly against rocks it had savagely pounded
earlier, while a contemporary moon covered the stationary
starlit spaces across the width of his bedroom window in
scant minutes. Arduous mental and metaphysical journeys left him with hours still to be spent. It was the devil's
own game. There was simply no using it up, unless he spent
all twenty-four hours at his desk. But work, for Henry, had
been a digression from the main business of living when
Stella had been here, and of course, Stella was still here.
Stella was here in the house. She walked about the garden.
She slipped through moonlit woods. If memories were not
total fabrication, Stella was here and now, but since no one
had ever seen a memory, they might well be, and perhaps
he had imagined his entire life. So back to Blavatsky and
Co., who understood the power of imagination and would
need no lengthy explanations if Henry broke the news that
he had not had a good night's sleep for months because
Stella was superimposed like a flame across his consciousness. Like the courthouse crowd Blavatsky would nod and
say comfortingly, Quite so. But the fact somehow did not

make for sanity and well-adjustedness, both of which he
would need in full measure if the next few transitional
weeks were not to turn out disastrous.

Henry's peon came in to tell him Madhav Rao was waiting to see him. Unlike most of Henry's constituency in
these parts there was no dilly-dally about Madhav Rao, a
plainsman somewhat scornful of the hills. He was excru-
ciatingly exact. He knew to the second when each of his
children had been born and all the coming landmarks in
their lives chronicled in their detailed horoscoped futures.
Chance did not figure in Madhav Rao's calculations and
only crisis could have pried him loose from his shop at two
p.m. on a weekday.

"What's the matter? Didn't your consignment of bilious
pills arrive?"

Henry saw the absurdity of his casual question when he
looked up to find the chemist and, he counted, fifteen others in the room. The leader of the delegation did not bother
to reply.

"I and my community have signed a petition." He handed
it to the peon, who handed it to Henry. "In this petition
we have stated that we do not want our children to learn
Christianity."

His own future upon him much sooner than he had
expected, Henry fervently wished he could put the Crofts
on the first rickshaw going downhill. He read the short
paragraph beginning "We respectfully pray" with sixteen
signatures under it. He read it twice and sat back in his
chair, going over it again. It was well known that when the
Collector had nothing to say he kept quiet until he had.
Henry recognized each man in the room. He was aware of
a somber collective determination, the somber droop of
moustaches, dark caps and turbans, darker eyes and but-

toned-up jackets. He was aware, too, of holding a tenuous balance between silence and excitable talk while he envisaged sixteen haggard Henrys petitioning Madhav Rao to save their children from perdition. His brief unstated acceptance of their plea, uncannily conveyed by the pause, converted it into a two-minute shared silence for a common cause. Tension visibly lowered. When he asked for details, the delegation, though not disposed to smile, answered charitably. They did not mind the school as such. English learning was necessary no doubt. Tantanna's exercises were first rate. But he must be knowing that in his predecessor's time Christianity had not been here, so what to say about teaching it?

Luckily for his predecessor Croft had been cooling his heels in jail and missionaries had not yet been given the freedom of this part of the Himalayas. Madhav Rao took pedantic Brahmanical charge of the interview, chalking it up for the reasonableness of his side that he and his community had not so far complained about A.D. being in school books instead of A.C. Henry suggested it was a bit late to raise that point now, but their petition had a point and he would look into it.

"Our other complaint is the sweeper's child in the class," said Madhav Rao.

Henry's mind leapt with alarm. Had Croft gone mad? He listened impatiently while the chemist took a piece of paper out of his pocket, put his glasses into it, coughed, sniffed, unfolded the paper and read in a language not immediately recognizable as English from the "late-late" Queen's Proclamation of 1858:

We do strictly charge and enjoin all those who may be in authority under us that they abstain from all inter-

ference with the religious belief or worship of any of
our subjects on pain of our highest displeasure.

"Yes, yes, I know," said Henry irritably.

Her son had come and gone, her grandson was on the
throne, but Victoria still reigned, and would be reigning
kings and possibly queens hence.

Two hours later he walked over to the Crofts and informed
the missionary in his best magisterial manner that there
could be no interference with religion and custom, and
especially not an inflammable combination of the two.
Before he was done he realized he should not have come
himself. Ultimatums were better delivered across a desk,
and his best magisterial manner was getting the worst of it
in the infernal racket with a carpenter hammering nails
into a contraption that looked like a large, elaborate swing,
the kind, Croft told him beaming, "we have on porches
back home." The "kids" would "get a kick out of it." Croft
was in shorts and shirt sleeves and was sawing at an enormous log with a fair amount of ease. The man had decided
calves and biceps. Henry raised his voice above the din.

"Mr. Croft, would you mind stopping your sawing and
that man's hammering for a few minutes?"

The hammer hit one last nail. Croft dusted wood shav-
ings off his shirt and offered, "We'll go in the house and let
Mrs. Croft get you some lemonade."

"I don't want lemonade," said Henry, fishing wood chips
out of his hair, "but let's go indoors by all means."

They got as far as the veranda where Lucille Croft was
airing clothes on wicker chairs. Towels hung along the
wooden balustrade. She took the trousers off two chairs for
them.

"The mildew is awful, isn't it? Nothing gets nice and dry

in this weather. I do hope you have good news of your wife and little girl, Mr. Brewster."

"Thank you," said Henry briefly.

He sat down facing Croft's underpants and repeated that government policy took no notice of untouchability.

"Now wait a minute," Croft leaned forward, "you passed a law against burning widows."

"After there had been a public agitation for it, and a demand was raised by educated opinion in this country."

"Well, while you're waiting for a demand, are you going to stand by and let these people be treated like pariahs?"

"Getting worked up won't help the issue, Mr. Croft. What you and I think about it is not going to alter their status by an iota."

"I don't know about that, sir," said Croft. "If you and I are not going to set an example, how is this ugly and undemocratic custom going to be uprooted?"

"I am not here to set examples and quite definitely not to uproot customs," said Henry wearily. "I am here to keep the peace and to collect revenue."

He found himself quoting Madhav Rao on the late-late Queen.

"I've got nothing but admiration for that great lady," Croft assured him. "God rest her soul. And for you sir, and the job you're doing. I don't want you to think I took this child in on an irresponsible impulse. Mrs. Croft brought it to my notice that the other children and their parents wouldn't like it. I have to tell you I acted against Mrs. Croft's better judgment. But I have not been able to identify Jesus with untouchability. I prayed for guidance and I believe the Lord wants me to go right ahead and keep this child in our class. I took him in. I can't throw him out."

"There's no need to throw him out. Just quietly remove

him. Your wife will tell you his father will be the first to understand. I'm afraid I must insist on it."

Lucille Croft, stuffing socks and shirts into a pillowcase to take indoors, agreed, "It's for the best, Marlowe. You don't want to start another native uprising, do you, with all the ghastly things that happened in the Mutiny?"

"There was ghastly savagery on both sides," said Henry, "but what you say is a case in point, Mrs. Croft. It would be very unwise of us to upset religious prejudices. Making soldiers use cartridges greased with pig's fat was an incredible disregard of their religious feeling. Your husband may not know the facts. Eighty-five men of the Third Cavalry refused to use them. And the way they were treated for refusing was another colossal blunder. They were court-martialed and sentenced to ten years' penal servitude. They were brought out under armed guards, still wearing their regimental uniforms, and the sentence was read out. Then they were publicly stripped of their uniforms and their arms, put in chains, and marched to jail. It was the ultimate insult to a soldier. Some of those men were the pride of their regiment, and all of them were loyal soldiers of the empire. A number of them cried out and begged the government not to disgrace them in this fashion. That was on the ninth of May, 1857. Armed rebellion began the day after that public humiliation. The cavalry and two infantry regiments broke into the jail to release their comrades. They set fire to their officers' houses, murdered every European they could lay hands on, and started on the road to more massacres in Delhi."

Lulu, startled but subdued, said, "What did I tell you, Marlow?"

"There's also some objection," Henry went on relentlessly, "to a class called Christian Endeavor."

Lulu confronted him with the bulging pillowcase. "It's not a class at all. It's singing and clapping. They're learning 'A Little Talk with Jesus Makes It Right All Right' and they love it."

"No harm in their singing and clapping," said Henry, getting up to go. "It's the songs the parents are objecting to. They don't want their children learning Christianity."

"I've just got it properly going," she burst out, after he had left.

"I know. I'm sorry Lulu. We'll get it going again later when we've got some support behind us."

"*When* later?" she demanded angrily, tears in her eyes, "In forty more years? *He's* never going to let us do anything."

"Now, Lulu," Marlowe put an arm around her, "I never told you it would be an easy life."

"I'm fed up with it. Why isn't anybody stopping sun saluting?"

Marlowe looked baffled. "Oh that. Miss Hansen's only here a little longer. It was a wonderful idea of yours to get her involved. She's great with the kids, and she's helping people get used to us. You've got plenty to do teaching reading and writing, Lulu. And once the D.M. hands down his decision we're going to have our hands full building the church."

"Does he look like a man who's going to hand down a decision to build a church?"

"It may take a while," he admitted.

She stared at him, incredulous, "Marlowe, it may take forever. Why can't you understand? I know his *type*. He's like the pen-pushing D.M.'s in Daddy's district, spouting about tenants' rights, local feelings, and all that tommyrot. What it means is he can't say boo to a goose. He can't even get over his stuck-up wife leaving him. *Now* what have I said wrong?"

It unnerved her to see him lower his big, muscle-bound body onto a bunch of vests, his shoulders sagging.

"There's one thing I won't let you do, Lulu, and that's give up hope about the church. The day we give up hope we might as well not be here." He straightened up and said more like himself, "The leadership is lacking. A fine man like Henry Brewster should be providing it, getting out there among the people and blazing a trail."

Lulu, draped with towels and a striped bathmat, held her tongue, or she would have said, Out where among which people, you must be losing your mind. With a sigh she got him off the vests and back to the woodshed.

The newspaper lay open on Brewster's desk in the library, with an empty coffee cup beside it. Anna found herself reading Tilak's statement to the press on his release:

> The Mandalay Jail is in the northwest corner of the Mandalay fort. I was never taken out of this building except on one occasion, for ten weeks, when cholera broke out in the jail. My cell was on the first floor and was twenty feet by twelve feet. . . . The compound around was about a hundred and thirty feet long and fifty feet wide. . . . Night and day the doors were fastened with heavy padlocks and at night my cell was also padlocked. Only when my time was nearly up did they cease to lock the door of the compound. The room that I have described was like a wooden cage. . . .

She looked up with a shiver at the room she stood in, measuring it with her mind's eye.

I had been sentenced to hard labor . . . in ten days I lost ten pounds in weight . . . the Government changed my sentence to simple imprisonment. . . . No newspapers or magazines were permitted. . . . After a time I was allowed books. Each book number was written on the frontispiece; I was never given ink to write with, only lead pencils, and they were sharpened beforehand. The only exception to this practice was when I wrote my monthly letter home. . . . Any matter which was not strictly related to family matters used to be cut out. On the slightest suspicion, even of a single word, the Superintendent used to make me write the whole letter again. I had no other contact with the outside world. . . .

The account was sedate, each bare fact austerely and impersonally recorded. Never could an "agitator" have been so faithful to the strict arithmetic of solitary confinement. What hope was there for the keepers of law and order now that pure arithmetic had become the language of sacrifice, and "sedition" could be born and reborn of plus and minus signs?

The prisoner had kept himself busy reading, and for a hundred and eighty days of his term, writing (with a lead pencil sharpened before it reached him) a commentary on the Bhagavad-Gita. He had examined the systems of Plato, Aristotle, Mill, Bentham, Green, Spencer, Comte, Kant, and Neitzsche, and compared them with those of Buddha, Ramanuja, and Confucius, and all of these with the teaching of the Bhagavad-Gita. And he had come to his own philosophic conclusions. He had had no time to worry about his health and, on the whole, it had been nothing to worry about, though . . .

my diabetes has become more acute than before and I have also lost five or six teeth. My deafness has increased, my sight has also been affected, and I cannot see properly now. In one word, the shadow of death is slowly creeping on me. Apart from this my mind and body are not much affected.

But the shadow of death had not crept on his writing or his following. The manuscript of *Gita Rahasya* lay with the Government, another caged lion awaiting release. And all night after his return people had streamed in to touch his feet with their foreheads and hear him say, "Six long years could not diminish my love for you."

Anna returned the books she had brought to their shelves and looked at the rows of books above and below without seeing a single one. She had choices to make, about what to read next, whether to stay in the library or go, think in great detail about the rest of her life or not think about it at all. Life had to move. Even the prisoner was practicing life and movement again, able to walk out of one four-walled room into another.

She started for home, then slowly retraced her steps, this time going to Brewster's office to ask him if he had more news of Tilak. His peon was not in the corridor and Brewster stood at the open window with his back to her, his hands hanging at his sides. At this rate his clothes would soon be too big for him, accentuating his lack of ruthlessness. She looked past him at a fragile mist lying in tatters over an apple tree, hanging in torn shreds from its branches. There was nothing whatever to remind her of the monstrous heat, the glare and dust of the wooden cage at Mandalay. Ridiculous of her to think, "My cell was on the first floor, twenty feet by twelve feet," of failing sight and hearing, or the huge enfeeblement of the shadow of death. She turned and went softly down the corridor.

As she left the house behind her it became easier to shake off her harrowing feeling of involvement with men and events she knew little or nothing of, chance encounters she would never meet or hear of again when she left Himapur. Himapur was a matter of three months in a lifetime. At once it jolted her to realize that fatal doses are infinitesimal, measured in grains. Matchless memories were made of sights and places seen just once. With a sinking feeling she recalled an unforgettable sky, and her eight-year-old gasp of delight when her father lowered it carefully with his hands and gave it to her as a present, saying, "Now it's yours forever."

E   I   G   H   T

◈

I t was decent of Henry Brewster to let Miss Hansen use
his library, and it took a load off Sir Nitin's mind. He
had felt responsible and uncomfortable about her free
hours. Europeans needed organized sport and organized leisure, with constant changes of clothes. Himapur did not
even have a bandstand on the ridge like other hill stations
where people could promenade in the evenings to the "Blue
Danube Waltz" and "Loch Lomond," and children could
buy ballons and popsicles and watch the bear-man and the
monkey-man. But thanks to the D.M. Miss Hansen could
occupy herself suitably with a good book from the official
residence, and he need not worry about her solitary excur-
sions. There would be fewer of them. He had fretted in
spite of Didi assuring him she would be more than a match
for any predatory male she might meet. Sir Nitin had not
expressed his own fears for her in quite those terms. Didi
had a way of taking bulls by their horns. Miss Hansen, she
had written to him, was used to going off by herself. In
Europe women thought nothing of it. They took hikes. They
scaled cliffs. They pedaled exhausting miles on bicycles.
Being single and female was no problem. She doesn't need
a chaperone, Potla. Incredible the amount of information
Didi had collected by hearsay about Miss Hansen. Every
letter had more of it, though "Your Rope," as she called it,

was and would remain a word in the dictionary for Didi. She had spent her entire insular life bossing her family more or less within Calcutta's city limits. She had only the vaguest idea what a hike was. She had never sat on a bicycle, and the only hill she had seen was on a poster at Calcutta's railway station, yet it did not prevent her being hearty and forthcoming about all these. In comparison, he was a mouse, one with advanced degrees and some experience of the world. A chance remark of Miss Hansen's had unwittingly reminded him, as she unwittingly did from time to time of things he hadn't thought about for years, that the world of bedtime stories, gods, demons, and old wives' tales he had been wrenched from when religious reform took over his family's life, still clung cosily to Didi. The Hindu Reformation had rolled over her head like a traveling rain cloud, dispensing its deluge somewhere else, leaving Didi warm and dry, snuggled up to myths and superstitions now celebrating their three-thousandth birthdays. For a second he felt like a sixty-year-old mouse without an umbrella.

Oh yes, Potla, she had written, I have been trying and trying to find out Miss Hansen's age since you are so anxious to know—why are you so anxious to know her age?—and I haven't been able to, because the people who introduced us had not known her long. I'm sure you are worried that people will be talking, depending on her age. From that point of view you have nothing to worry about because in any case she's a European. So how should her age concern anyone? The Banerjis are big gossips but they know me. Would I send you a frivolous assistant? They have met her so they must know she has had a good upbringing. Forget about her age. You never could tell anybody's age. Don't you remember how you made the Vice Principal of the Jagat

Narain Girls' High School cry when you asked her how her grandson was doing in the provincial police? Not only was she unmarried (with no hope whatsoever of marrying) but you thought you were addressing her mother. She was very upset. She kept asking me afterwards, Do I really look as old as my mother? All these fiascos could be avoided if you met more human beings, work is all very well. Funny Potla. I found Miss Hansen extremely sincere and courageous, though, of course, very tall. I hope the cook isn't cheating you right and left. I know these hillmen. Why don't you have a frank talk with Miss Hansen about white sugar? I am glad to hear she has of her own accord stopped serving fricadella, but what is the harm in a little fricadella? You are too stern and stuck in your plants. No one would believe the sweet cuddly baba you used to be, smiling away when Mama's friends picked you up and pestered you with hugs and kisses. Your loving Didi. P.S. I will let you know in case I do manage to find out her age.

Sir Nitin's choice of books would have been different from Miss Hansen's. He opened the one she had left on the dining table. It was a life of Tulsidas, by some obscure biographer, published twenty years earlier. It would probably be a collector's item since he had heard of no other biography in English of the author of the Hindi Ramayana. He was glad Miss Hansen had graduated from B.C. to the sixteenth century, but it was a pity she was not more curious about modern India when the country was trying to cast off ignorance and make strides under British rule, though he noticed with relief that Miss Hansen now moved freely between the past and present tense and managed more complicated sentence structures. Not that India hadn't a great deal to teach Britain, but in her present fallen condition she was destined to sit at the feet of England for many,

many years, or so he had believed since he'd heard a great Bengali patriot say so in a stirring speech in 1877 soon after Victoria assumed the title of Empress of India. It was disconcerting that the great Bengali patriot now sounded like Mrs. Croft, if she had had a noble-sounding sentiment in her head and the ability to express it. He recalled that the reason given in that speech for sitting many years at the feet, etc., was to learn Western art and science. A speck of rage alighted on the tip of Sir Nitin's mind. He brushed it off as Miss Hansen came into the room.

"So here is the book," she said, "I was looking for it to return to Mr. Brewster's house. But if you want to read it I can take it back later."

Sir Nitin, restored to his fallen condition, explained kindly that he came of a reformed family, leading members of the Brahmo Samaj, whose founder had set up the very first Western-style college in Calcutta. Myths and legends had their place in a heritage, but his own parents had been particular about giving him a modern English education.

"Didi told me there is no difference between the Brahmo Samaj and a Christian padre," said Miss Hansen, putting the book into a shapeless cotton bag she had slung over her shoulder. " 'So what's all the hoo-ha about reform,' she said. 'They might as well call themselves second-class Christians and be done with it.' "

"Not a very respectful way to refer to a historic movement," said Sir Nitin. "My sister was educated in a convent school, but to hear her talk one would never know it."

"Yes, she told me she never fitted in. She could not wait to come home every afternoon, pull off her uniform, her shoes and her socks, bundle them up, throw them high in the air and become herself as the clock struck four."

Plans for Departure

"A personality cannot be cast off like a shoe or a sock, Miss Hansen, whatever my sister may have told you. The clock struck four indeed. It's a wonder she didn't think she was a pumpkin turning into a coach."

Miss Hansen beamed as she tied her head up in a spotted kerchief. "About you she said, 'My baby brother Potla only has Beowulf for a myth, not much comfort in his old age. It terrified him out of his wits when he was wee.' "

"Well really," said Sir Nitin coldly. "She seems to have done a lot of talking over a cup of tea." Over the same cup she had discovered Miss Hansen's sincerity and courage.

Miss Hansen went off in a lighthearted mood, leaving Sir Nitin fidgeting at his desk in Standard One where at a quarter to nine a.m. Grendel the evil monster came down from the moors to tear down the doors of King Hrothdar's palace with his bare hands and devour the king's guests. Two pages later Beowulf wrenched off the monster's arm. At nine-thirty Isaac laid his curly head on a block and hoary Abraham stood with ax up-raised under the eye of the bearded God afloat on a cloud. Foreign gods and devils did not get digested like tales told by grandmothers patting one to sleep to the rhythm of once upon a time the ocean was churned by the gods to recover the lost nectar of immortality. Foreign gods and devils lived and breathed in climates of their own though the classroom temperature was a scalding 100°, and outside, crows hopped hopefully near ayahs and bearers who squatted with tiffin carriers waiting to spoon rice and *dal* into their babas during the lunch break. In the classroom foreigners won blood-stained victories and foreign virtue triumphed with pictures to prove it. Teacher in a frock, due to the drop of English blood in a foremother's vein, rapped knuckles with a ruler and instructed, "Don't slouch, Knitting, three times three makes what?"

and "Stand up when you answer, Knitting, my but y'all are a cheeky bunch."

Years later Nitin Basu, well on his way to making a lasting impact on his generation, knew that Nirvana was neither the art and culture, the law and order of his masters, nor the fire-breathing nationalism of his province. It was Work. And so long as he was left in peace to carry on his work uninterrupted, the gods and demons outside it could prance their toes and whiskers off.

Anna, with her sling bag, her kerchief, and books in disorder at her feet, was sitting in her favorite chair rereading parts of the Tulsidas biography when her host came in.

"There you are. Would you care to join me in a cup of tea today, or would you prefer to be left alone?"

"Usually alone." she admitted. "Time goes quickly when I am here."

Time—its utterly individual pace and passage.

"But I would like to join you today," she accepted.

He looked barely held together by a taut outer covering. Remove his skin and his bones would collapse, which bones shouldn't if there was a sturdy, happy skeleton binding them. Tea arrived and was put down in front of her by the bearer, she and Henry assuming a man's and a woman's role on either side of it without a word spoken. This was no place for Scandinavian debate, so she poured, telling him she found her book's subject a mysterious figure.

"Some of these books belonged to my predecessor. He donated them to the house. I haven't read that one."

"Then you cannot tell me if this Tulsidas really treated his wife as the author says."

"Poets and writers make notoriously bad husbands," said Henry and gave her several examples.

"But he was not a bit like Dickens," said Anna. "He was too devoted to his wife. Too much in love."

Had she imagined the wary flicker in his eyes, the fear of recognition?

"What do you mean by too much?"

"He could not bear to be parted from her though they were children when they married and always together. He would make scenes every time she wanted to visit her parents. He said he could not live a day without her."

"Stuffy of him," said Henry, "and suffocating for her."

"The wife's feeling exactly. So one day while he was out, she packed up and went home. When he came back and found her gone, he thought he would go raving mad, and set off to bring her back."

"How did he know where she'd gone?"

"Where else but to her parents?" asked Anna. "There was nowhere else to go. Now, to get to her village he had to cross a river and he nearly drowned crossing it against the current. At her parents' house, he had to climb up a creeper to reach her room. It was a big struggle but finally he could succeed. And there she was."

Henry seemed absorbed.

"But the point of the story is," continued Anna, "that the raft he used to cross the river had been a floating corpse, and the creeper he climbed to reach her room was a live snake. He did not know. And when she told him, he did not care."

"I see what you mean. One can picture his—demented—frame of mind."

"It filled her with horror," said Anna.

"And she left him," Henry finished for her.

Anna replenished their cups. "A wife seldom leaves, especially in the sixteenth century. And then she was a pious woman."

"So the story has a conventional ending in spite of all the drama in between," said Henry.

"The drama is yet to come. She tells her husband she is disgusted and ashamed of his love. A passion like his cannot be wasted on a mortal frame. If he can endanger his life and be lost to reason and sanity for a woman, then he is on the path, if only he can see it, to the love of God."

Henry had the tight, drawn look of a man whose temples ached and throbbed. She was shocked at the effect of her words.

It was an interesting story, he remarked. He knew Tulsidas had gone down in history as a saint after he had written the Ramayana, but he didn't know this was how he had come to write the epic. In a way the whole exercise had been a waste of earthly love. Hadn't his wife realized what she was losing? A lot of women would have been vastly flattered instead of disgusted and ashamed. He left Anna to explore the higher bookshelves. When she came out he was speaking to the gardener about manure. They fell into a comfortable stride.

"Where are you going to educate your daughter?" Anna asked.

There was a pause before he answered. "I don't know yet."

He asked her when she and Sir Nitin would be leaving.

"The actual date? He has not decided yet."

"Please tell him I shall be glad to help with arrangements. Resthouses have to be booked for the journey down."

"So soon?"

"Arrangements take time. What will you do after you leave Himapur?"

"I have not thought so far ahead."

He walked with her down the slope as far as the sentry

post at the bottom of the incline. The sentry saluted smartly and Henry nodded to him.

"The Balkan situation is deteriorating," he said.

"When is it not?"

"It's worse than ever. The news is not good."

"No," said Anna.

The sentry continued to stand at attention, staring past their heads.

"I suppose I should be making some plans too," said Henry, abruptly adding, "Stella is not coming back."

They must have looked, she thought afterward, like fixtures in a three-pointed tableau, the sentry rigid and expressionless, her own emotional reaction writ large, and Henry's features as natural and normal as pain would allow.

"I'm so sorry," was all she could say, aware of its enormous inadequacy.

"I was expecting it."

One also expected death all one's life, and was taken just as unawares by it, so what good was expecting? He must have preferred his threadbare hopes to the finality of this news. He said good-by and walked slowly up the slope. She knew how slowly, turning to watch him. She was convinced she had cried out, "Henry, wait for me!" But his retreating back and the sentry's impassive face as he chewed a blade of grass assured her she had not.

She forced herself to think of the Balkans. Nicholas's last letter, from London where he was now posted, was full of distant drama. Crowned heads exchanged telegrams reminding each other of the tender ties of blood and sentiment that bound them. Governments burned the midnight oil trying to keep the Austro-Serbian crisis from spreading. Diplomatic pouches carried sensible proposals urging negotiation, mediation, arbitration. But how could they be in earnest if everyone was still arming, she thought. Turn the pouches inside out and miniscule memories of old scores still to be settled must be falling out of secret linings with different messages across them. And if rehearsals were so far advanced as Nicholas seemed to think, someone had only to push a button and war would come on like clock-work—or by pure chance if a patrol went up the wrong road on a fortified frontier and ran into an enemy patrol. Nicholas had sounded pessimistic, overworked, and bone-weary. His letter rang with the hoofbeats of imperial cavalries at military maneuvers and orders for mobilization— still partial, of course—which did not amount to declarations of war. But the war nobody wanted seemed to be coming along as fast as if everybody needed it for survival. It was unbelievable that two peace-loving emperors who wrote each other affectionate reams, and called each other Willy and Nicky, couldn't control their war machines. And now the letter she was going to write involved her in entirely new mental agonies.

Plants get drunk like humans, Anna wrote in her actual letter to Nicholas. One drink of whiskey made a mimosa straighten up and look bright and eager. Another drink made it drowse and droop. The third drink made it drunk and folded its little leaves. But after four hours' sleep it shook off its hangover and was fresh and perky again. I am enchanted with this particular experiment I am writing up. It plainly shows, as Sir Basu says, that plants have animal (or human) traits, but so far hardly anyone in the scientific community accepts his finding. He says botanists in the West may accept that a tree feels the woodsman's axe, but he wonders if he can persuade them about the tortures peas go through when boiled. I told him I didn't think a single Dane, or Englishman, would believe it. Meat and potatoes every day is not the best diet for revolutionary thinking. I myself find it quite possible to believe that vegetables are on their way, in who knows how much time, to becoming human, though he says this will, of course, be for future biologists to research. But look at the evidence. Already there is a plant, again the clever mimosa, who knows how to dodge a cow when it comes trampling. It shrinks and closes into itself faster than a snail or a turtle. And there are Sir Basu's findings about vegetables besides. The carrot is highly excitable and the most reacting of them all. Celeries don't get so easily agitated. I've come to the conclusion I'm a carrot and you're a celery. I'm not writing at all in English this time, as I have too many things on my mind, you, myself, the Balkans, and everything here in Himapur. Henry told me today that the beauteous Stella is not coming back. The uncertainty had been a strain on him and I should have thought anything would be better than going on groping in thin air, but he has taken it like news of a death. I see a priest emerging out of that pale fire, a consuming religious dedication taking the place of his love for Stella. There is a lot of plain human goodness in him which must find an outlet. Feelings as powerful as his for Stella can't be snuffed out like a candle. If they were, the air around the candle would catch fire in the dark. They can't just disappear. He says most women would think themselves lucky to have a husband who loved them "too much." I put myself in Stella's place and tried to imagine myself at the mercy of such searing constancy, and to tell you the truth, dearest Nicholas, I felt a little afraid. Perhaps she was afraid of him and had to escape him to remain human. Talking might help him if he would only talk. I think he may now, though his melancholy has been like a wall in the way of real communication. Trespassers will be prosecuted. Yet I have a great and growing desire to trespass.

And only after she had posted her letter did she realize she had forgotten to say anything about the far continent called Europe.

Henry read her handwriting with reluctant ease. He was familiar with her English, with her French, and along with dearest Nicholas, he was privy to her thoughts. Her letters would ordinarily have been opened, read and resealed at the post office, but the junior police officer stationed here couldn't read French. Her correspondence added little to his dossier on Anna. Her dossier on him seemed better filled. It would have been altogether safer from the point of view of secrecy if the man she wrote to had been an anonymous Dane, off the operative map of the world, instead of someone in the British Foreign Office. Henry found it burdensome enough to be carrying official responsibility at such a time without the details of his private torment and the reasons for it being graphically conveyed to a person close to persons in power. Diplomats were notoriously well connected. The missionary, who could have been much more of a nuisance than Anna, was busy with his school, his soul-saving activity at a standstill for the time being' and carpentry to the fore. He wrote few letters. "I have to keep reminding Lulu she must make friends," he had last written to someone in Kansas he called Hank, making Henry shudder with relief at the fate he had escaped by not being born American. The sentence amounted to a resting place in their tug-of-war about land for a church. The day La Croft made friends, manna would fall like hail from the heavens,

the population of Himapur would push and shove to learn
Christianity and the District Magistrate would grant land
for the church with a fanfare of trumpets and drums. He
would happily cut the ribbon to inaugurate it and make all
the joyful noises required. But none of this could happen
while La Croft raised solid phalanxes of hostility every time
she opened her mouth. He and his successors could all go
about their business without a care while they waited for
the years to pass and for La Croft to grow too feeble for
venom. But Henry could see no such peaceable stalemate
arising in Anna's thoughtsharing with Nicholas. Unfortunately, prying into the District Magistrate's state of soul
or his liverish condition would not be reason enough to
deport her. Even Robert Pryor, born suspicious, would need
a better reason.

Henry put the letter back in its envelope. The bearer had
forgotten to close the curtains earlier. He could see the
shadows cast by the cook's dim swinging lantern and hear
the soft crunch of his shoes on gravel as he made his way
to the servants' quarters. Between the swaying lantern and
his own determination to rise from his chair and go to bed,
there was a long, strange lapse. Time settled silently and
faithfully as a deaf dog at his feet, unwilling to stir while
his master sat. Until this evening's offering from Anna had
arrived nights were beginning to be more tolerable. When
he got up to pull the curtain cord he heard the sinuous
sound of rain. He was no longer sure of the progress he was
beginning to make toward sounder sleep. But by the time
he was in bed a frantic downpour rattled the roof, blacked
out moon, stars, and all vestige of unease, and he slept
dreamlessly. Nights later, waking to a curdled moonlit rec-
tangle of sky, bits of the letter came back—"feelings so
powerful as his for Stella," "to tell you the truth, dearest

Nicholas, I felt a little afraid," "I have a growing desire to trespass." He had to summon all his determination not to shout and rave. When he felt calm enough to drowse, he had the distinct feeling his life was over and his death had just begun.

Anna had never seen Madhav so concentrated, yet so peculiarly lost to the world, as he went back and forth between her and The Camera like a terrier in an alert and efficient sort of trance. The picture-taking process had swallowed him and his camera. They had dissolved into each other and become One. It brought the whole business of mystical union and peace of mind within hitting range. It was largely a matter of homework. She could probably get there if she tried over the next few lifetimes. The one as Anna Hansen didn't hold out much hope. All night yesterday's sunlight had lain on the rose-purple rhododendron bordering Henry's driveway. No effort would rid her of it. She would see it for the rest of her life, every time she looked out of a window on the other side of the world at alien grass and flowers, every time she walked down alien garden paths.

Back at her side Madhav arranged stray strands of her hair with careful fingers, dampened the collar of her blouse with a dash of water and patted it down. He stepped back to survey the effect with an absorption so uncompromising that her distraught and scattered energies flew together and composed themselves in sheer obedience. She knew she had been flung by forces beyond her control into a harmony so fleeting and complex that if a bell had rung she would have collapsed. Madhav vanished under The Camera's black shroud but Anna's composure held. If she did not move, wounds would heal, friendship would flower, and answers would be serenely, miraculously delivered.

Madhav reappeared to cover the lens with its cap. His eldest son, who had been stage-managing the scenery behind Anna, offered his father a plate and Madhav slid it into position. Off came the lens cap and an eloquent, upright index finger worked its way out from under the shroud to show he was ready at last. But Anna wasn't. Madhav's long disappearance had chloroformed her. Her fleeting harmony had become permanent. One foot had gone to sleep. Her arms, legs, blouse, and neck were soldered to her torso. Her face was locked into plaster of Paris with marbles for eyes. The backdrop Madhav had ordered for her had a tree. Her chair was against it, and overhead a bird of no recognizable species sat sideways on a bough. She felt she had been crowned with one of Marie Antoinette's architectural hair styles, the one that had most entranced Versailles. It had had a window opening out of three feet of curled and powdered wig to reveal a singing canary in a gleaming gold cage.

"A lover of nature like you must be framed by the beauty of nature," Madhav had laid down when they had (in a manner of speaking) discussed the backdrop.

His voice issued like a muffled bugle at sundown, "Do not smile, Tantanna. You are serious by character."

This, too, had been decreed beforehand. In his usual authoritarian fashion Madhav had ruled out the head-tilted, sweet-smile pose suitable for most unwed females and matrons with pleasure-loving dispositions. But even if he had changed his mind it would by now have taken a crane to tilt her head and undo her face into a smile. She looked forbiddingly into The Camera for a tense count of ten. While

Madhav busied himself with afterbirth preparation and the eldest son put the tree away, Anna massaged her neck and exchanged an understanding glance with Stella Brewster, whose hair had acquired the black gloss of cherries. Acquaintance had given Stella a captive look of tender, wistful beauty. Maybe posterity would recognize herself as human and vulnerable too, thought Anna, when she hung on that wall among bridal pairs, landowners, and other camera-struck gentry.

They sat down to their ritual tea. Lowering her voice, as she and Madhav did when they talked about Tilak, although there was no third person in the room and precious few outside it, Anna asked, "What will happen to Tilak's book, the commentary on the Bhagavad-Gita he wrote in jail?"

He shrugged. He had no idea.

"It is nothing to do with politics," said Anna, "They cannot call it seditious."

As to that, Tilak had made the Bhagavad-Gita seditious before he ever went to jail, Madhav informed her. According to his interpretation, the split second when one jumped over one's mind and hit Realization was not the end of the story. One had to hurry back from private bliss to public duty and spend the rest of one's life making the world a better place. A very energetic man, Tilak.

"What is so seditious about that?" asked Anna.

"Tza! How do you not understand? If you are changing the world and English judges and juries are not liking the change, it is sedition. In any case the trouble starts with the Gita itself. Sri Krishna is standing on a battlefield. He does not mince words. Has he got time to waste? The armies are ranged. Their horses are stamping, their elephants are trumpeting. He orders "Fight!" Why? Because God created battle and armor, the sword, the bow, and the dagger to fight for justice and righteousness. It is all written there, Tantanna. And Tilak is fanning the flames by saying that Realized people must forget about sitting and meditating in caves. They must rise from the lotus position and carry on the fight."

"I hope he did not mention all those weapons in his commentary," said Anna, worrying about English judges and juries.

But it was plain common sense, she agreed, that salvation should not be a one-way ride, with the fortunate ones passing off into selfish antisocial bliss, leaving the rest of humanity in the lurch. Why hadn't anyone thought of it before? Why shouldn't a Realized shoemaker or poet make better shoes and poetry instead of spending his enlightenment being blissful in a cave? With his hair, his beard and his eyelashes growing until they touched the ground, added Madhav. There were stories of yogis who, when they heard a human voice after unknown spans of years, had to lift their eyelashes off the ground with the backs of both hands to see who was standing there. Much more useful, he nodded, to be serving mankind in a shoeshop than getting into the back-breaking struggle of lifting up eyelashes at remote high altitudes. Tilak had therefore made caves out-of-date. And Madhav's father, an ardent admirer of Tilak, had devoted his entire life before and after Realization to the service of the PWD and his joint family. How he had loved his children and his brothers' children and with what devotion he had guarded their morals. Madhav grew misty with reverent recollection. He, his real brothers and his cousin brothers could never forget his father hissing "Eyes must shut!" when they were at the bioscope and "Eyes to open!" when sights forbidden to adolescents had passed off the screen. "Tza what hisses! And how he thrashed us if we disobeyed," Madhav nostalgically reminisced. "Such fatherly care." As for Tilak's book, writings on philosophy were so philosophical as to make them appear quite harmless. So the book would probably be published. But they would catch him again for his *Kesari* and *Maratha* articles, which again were nothing but common sense.

"All he keeps saying is that the King and the administration are two separate things. The kingship is like Brahma, eternal and unchanging. We have nothing against kingship or queenship. Let it be. We are full of respect. But who rules India? Not the King. It is his servants, the Viceroy, the governors, the collectors, the policemen. These fellows must go. What is their business here? We will look after our own affairs. And why should we petition for every small thing? Why, why Tantanna?" he barked.

"You should not," said Anna, calm and firm.

"You are Danish," said Madhav with relief, and subsided.

But even though Danish, with no colonies, and of no consequence in world affairs, she was aware of the caged lions in boxes in the corridor outside Madhav's suffocating studio, biding their time, like Tilak's book, to spring again. And now that the last frontier had been crossed and metaphysical freedom was not enough, no one would be safe from the charge of sedition. Next time the country would be tried and jailed.

"Bombs are homemade things," said Madhav, his eyes roaming restlessly around the room. "Picric acid, an empty bottle, what is there? I could make one myself."

Unreasonable anxiety gripped Anna as she left his studio. Outside a breeze cooled her face and lifted the ends of her hair. A rickshaw, weighted with mounds of soft flesh in spangled silk, came out of the mist toward her, turned right, and toiled past. Pumped by the rhythmic clatter of coolie breath it took a sudden spurt forward. A silvery laugh fell out and lay shriveled like chocolate wrapping in the street.

Henry was at his desk in the library going through its drawers. He apologized for the mess, and for his presence, as if it were her room, slammed the drawers shut, and said he was just leaving.

"No, please. I only came to ask if there is anything I can do, in case this news from your wife affects your plans."

"I have no plans, Anna."

"You are not thinking of going away then?"

He got up and paced the room with this hands in his pockets, a man accustoming his limbs and his shoulder blades as much as his mind to a new situation.

"There was a time a few years ago when I was ready to quit and knew exactly what I wanted to do with my life. But Stella was against it, and openings don't stay open."

"She wanted to stay in India?"

"She was well brought up and took her duties seriously. I couldn't. Apart from the rights and wrongs of being here, there's no future in it. I'm convinced we'll have to clear out in my lifetime."

It might have been true of other lifetimes, Anna saw long afterwards, had Englishmen not been called up to fight for king and country, some of them twice over. At the moment the only accomplished departure was Stella's, and it was all wrong, since Stella was the one who had wanted to stay. Any other seemed most unlikely, especially on a grand imperial scale.

"I never could convince Stella," said Henry. "She didn't believe in a changing world."

And yet, one fine day, Stella had changed her own, without a backward glance at the wilderness she was leaving behind.

"The world is changing," Anna agreed, "but not fast enough."

"At least we should recognize the changes we see."

Henry sat down in the nearest chair, bunched and uncomfortable because he had forgotten to take his hands out of his pockets, and recited, " 'By the Sun that warms me, by the Earth that nourishes me, before God, by the blood of my ancestors, on my honor and on my life, I will from this moment till my death be faithful to the laws of this organization, and I will always be ready to make any sacrifice for it.' "

"Which organization?"

"It's the oath of the Black Hand," he said, "the Serbian secret society responsible for the Austrian Archduke's murder. One of the murder crew was taken prisoner and they got it out of him. The day any occupier meets with that spirit and can't match it life for life, the game is up."

"Can a few fanatics really wind up the game?"

"It depends what you mean by fanatic. In the Middle Ages it meant devotee. This man in the Archduke conspiracy considered himself an upright, patriotic citizen. He described his leader as a gentle, retiring person who was doing his duty training assassins, distributing bombs and pistols, and dispensing cyanide to be swallowed as soon as the deed was done."

"There are not so many Khudirams here," she said.

"I see you've heard about a case I dealt with. But you're right, Anna, that's not why we'll leave. There's no shortage of hangmen or ropes and there aren't many bomb-throwing patriots. Nor can a few individuals defeat a system. It was myself I didn't like the look of as I watched the boy strung up. And I am not alone. There is another England, one that doesn't preside over executions on soil where it has no right to be in the first place. There's a new world in the making at home. I wanted to be present at its birth." He took his hands out of his pockets, unclenched his fists and said, incredulous, "But I could never make Stella see it. It was like being, well, on opposite sides in the American Civil War."

"With you as Abraham Lincoln?"

He looked abashed and rejected any claim to moral superiority. "I have no illusions of grandeur. That's my trouble."

But now Anna saw the sense of it. Stella had taken a political stand instead of a lover. When two people had an uncrossable barrier the size of an empire between them, one of them could only retreat, for reasons, oddly enough, of keeping the flag flying. There was nothing more to know about the Brewster marriage. A Church-of-England wife is not the wife of Tulsidas. Stella had had views no one had heard, and she had taken them to their logical conclusion. Anna went to the window where nothing was clear. Stella's fruit-loaded tree was a blur. The rest of the garden was fading away. Shadows sleepwalked through the mist to shadowy destinations.

"I suppose if there's a war, your plans will be affected," said Henry.

Anna turned slowly from the window to say the news from Europe was depressing, which did not amount to an answer.

"A friend of mine was at a party in Paris for the Grand-duchess Anastasia whose husband, you know, is head of the Tsar's armed forces. Nicholas's letter said the Grand-duchess talked excitedly about the Russian empire taking action if its blood brothers, the Serbians, are threatened. She actually told her host, 'Our armies will meet in Berlin. We will wipe out Germany and Austria. And you will get back Alsace-Lorraine.' Yet everyone knows the Tsar himself wants peace."

Though Nicholas, she added, was not so sure. He had written that war would have its uses for the peaceful Tsar. It would clear his way to Constantinople and the Dardanelles, and take the nuisance of workers' strikes off the boil at home. Military bands were practicing "La Marseillaise" to welcome the French President at Krasnoe Selo, and the autocrat of all the Russias would stand to attention when it was played though it was banned in his empire. You couldn't tinkle it on your own private piano if the tinkle could be heard in the street, and cossacks were battering workers in St. Petersburg for singing it, but war would give Russia an ally that marched to it. Russia was mobilizing. So was every other Power, though each one wanted peace. And with the mounting fervor for peace looking so wildly warlike, England's navy had to be prepared too.

"It is not at all clear to me," said Anna, "who wants war and who wants peace. My head is completely confused. Why do countries have to be powers, and why do Powers have to be Great? And what have emperors' follies to do with me?"

Henry got up and came toward her. There was a glitter of angry determination about his face that might have been tears. He took her firmly by the wrists. "None of those things are very clear to me either. But we're not alone, Anna. There's such a tremendous future waiting for people like us—." He dropped her wrists with the rest of his sentence.

"Is there, Henry?"

"I'm greatly in your debt," he continued quietly. "It has

been comforting to know there was someone else in the house. It's a big house to rattle around in by oneself. I've never even thanked you. I shall miss you when you leave Himapur."

The directness of Anna's blue-gray glance, and his own regard for her, ruled out any major diversion from the truth. He meant what he said, but she must realize she had to leave. The dates and times of departures had to be decided, the sooner the better. Summer visitors must get on with their lives. A rising fever to be alone possessed him as they walked down the slope together.

The heat and cold of fever, the sweating and shivering, made sleep impossible, which for one reason or another was impossible anyway. Tonight his bedroom framed a sky of solid black. The moon at its most linear hung somewhere else. Between shivering bouts the unbroken dark was restful. His mind wandered with the utmost clarity. Good-by dear Valkyrie, with your shining hair and eyes, and your tramping feet. Go to your dearest Nicholas. War or no war, it is time. Time for those you found here to be left to their natural fate. I shall think of you and "Sir Basu" on your way down. He will do justice to his rupee's worth of mutton chops, chicken curry, and tea at the first resthouse, even if you don't. In case it is cold, two armfuls of wood will do for the fireplace. There is no view worth the name, but just before rain the sky is sorrowful with mauve-and-purple bruises that will touch your uncorrupted heart. At any rate your time here is up. It's no business of yours whether the silence mutters or rages round me. You're wrong if you think religion, of which you accuse me, will come to my rescue. The planets will continue to spin in

the void. If there are such things as saints and sinners—
and not merely all of us bound by each other's good and
evil—they stay in their separate compartments.

Don't think I haven't looked for relief in the scriptures,
but Jehovah says one thing, Allah another. Did we really
need these voices in the desert, more coolie loads to stag-
ger under? And Croft is welcome to spread the word about
his only Son of God. You can't know how angry all "mission" makes me. You were born nine centuries after Denmark gave up raiding, colonizing, and lusting after worlds
to conquer. If I am ever driven to belief, it will have to be
Madhav Rao's law of moral consequences, which catches
up, as it has with me.

Blavatsky, however bogus, was dead right on one point.
The entire bagful of tricks is either sublime religion or rank
superstition. Why should it be superstition when Aeolus
ties and unties the winds, and religion when the Jews see
their Lord God flying upon the wings of the wind with
smoke coming out of his nostrils and fire out of his mouth?
Why was the oracle at Delphi that told the Greeks to sacrifice to the winds when they saw Xerxes' fleet sail into
view any different from Elijah looking for the Lord in the
wind and the earthquake? Jupiter hurled thunderbolts and
lightning. So did the Lord God of Abraham and Jacob: "The
Lord thundered from heaven, and the most High uttered
His voice. And He sent arrows and scattered Saul's armies;
lightning, and discomfited them." Yes, I have been reading
the Bible, sitting each evening where your form is now
imprinted in your favorite chair. This, too, I have to live
with. Forms don't fade and disappear. I will see you sitting
in that chair years from now, gesturing with your long,
articulate hands. I can still after all this time see the proud
little tilt of Stella's chin at the execution. But I was saying,

Jesus, too, "arose and rebuked the wind and the raging of the water, and they ceased and there was calm."

It was the wind and the weather substituting for revelation. It still does, as you well know, Valkyrie. I've seen the authentic glow in your cheeks after a day in the open, with the breezes blowing around you. You understand much better than most that the wind in the heath and the light on the high hills are no more than the pulse beating and the blood coursing through you from the climb. There are no altars up there. So the love of God can never be the answer to my sleeplessness. If I'm to sleep easy now, I'll have to put my own disordered mind in irons and bring it to heel. For the time being I have no goal but this.

I wish I shared your view about divine intervention in my life, but there's hard labor involved in suing for it with no pious wife to put me on the path. So there can be no nimble hand-held leap in the dark for me, Valkyrie. If the best-behaved of us are supposed to be sinners, how do I rate divine grace? I am better qualified to join the desperate. I have the required amount of zeal for the wrong causes. The rules for admission to the Black Hand fit me like a glove. They were designed for those who want neither glory nor personal profit, and "Every member on entering the organization must realize that by this act he forfeits his own personality." I could ask for nothing more. The oath is a bit melodramatic, and I don't much like the idea of taking it by the light of a candle at a table covered with a black cloth, with a crucifix, a dagger, and a revolver on it—but after the oath, life is short and simple. All that matters is the execution of a chosen victim and one's own immediate suicide.

He spent the next two days in bed. In a dream he marched fevered miles down a poplar-lined road with others like himself, all of them singing. On the third day he was up and watched himself deal efficiently with arrears of work. The last heavy downpour had disturbed a hill, an annual event in some part of the territory he administered. In summer it was the rains, in winter the snow, and spring and autumn felt the blast of blizzards higher up. Tons of rocky soil had been deposited across a road leading into the interior. Leaning lightly on his walking stick he stood reviewing the damage. No human being or animal had been injured in the landslide, and it was a remarkable piece of luck it had not blocked the main road, which would have held up visitors who had not yet left for the plains. There had been very little damage to the main road, and if luck held, all would be well.

Anna laid the sheet of cyclostyled print on the counter and tried to rub the smudges off her fingers.

"The meeting is in two days," said Madhav, informing her she was to attend it.

The announcement hailing Tilak's return owed some of its joyous abandon to mixed metaphors. Esteemed-by-the-people was life-giving rain after drought. His suffering shone in the people's hearts like the polestar on a winter night. His sacrifice was the sùn on their fields. He was teacher turned liberator. He was their father and their mother. The citizens of Himapur joined the whole country in welcoming him home, especially on behalf of imprisoned patriots and journals that had been suspended by the obnoxious Press Act. Below the welcome, bits of Tilak's speech at the 1906 session of the Indian National Congress had been put together in a big smudge. Anna read:

This government does not suit us. We are not going to sit down quiet. If you mean to be free, you can be free. We shall not give them assistance to collect revenue and keep peace. We shall not assist them in fighting beyond the frontiers or outside India with Indian blood and money. We shall not assist them in carrying out the administration of justice. We shall have our own courts, and when the time comes we shall not pay taxes. Can you do that by your united efforts? If you can, you are free from tomorrow. Some gentlemen who spoke this evening referred to half bread as against the whole bread. I say I want the whole bread and immediately . . .

"Do you call that a speech?" Sir Basu picked it up by its right-hand corner and held it gingerly between the tips of his thumb and forefinger. "It was no better when I heard it delivered. That such a tone and sentiments should come out of the Congress, one of the noblest monuments to British rule!"

Anna had to admit Sir Basu's chit-chat was more like speeches than Tilak's speech.

He handed it back to her across the excellent mutton curry the cook had produced for dinner. It glistened with oil. It was redolent with spices. Mellowly he recalled that the fourth, seventh, eighth, and, if he remembered correctly, the eleventh and thirteenth sessions of the Congress had opened on Mr. Gladstone's birthday. The delegates had given three cheers for him before getting down to business, and had sent him a telegram of good wishes. He died the following year, and the President of the fourteenth Congress, in 1898 that was, had paid him a most beautiful tribute. The meeting had passed a resolution expressing its grief, and sent a telegram of sympathy to Mr. Herbert Gladstone.

"Why?" asked Anna.

"Mr. Gladstone was the greatests statesman of modern times, Miss Hansen. His death was an irreparable loss to the British empire and the civilized world."

To which apparently the Danes did not belong, as there was not a glimmer of intelligent response.

"I trust you are not going to this Tilak affair," he said.

"I will see how the weather is."

The following week she climbed a flight of stairs, stepping into pools and puddles left by other feet. Muddy water oozed out of her boots, the hem of her skirt was soaked, and her umbrella had not kept her dry. A jubilant hum of human noise had found its level between the paraffin lamps and the rain. The dais was festooned with Tilak's mottos, "Freedom is my birthright and I will have it" in saffron letters, "Militancy, not Mendicancy" in green. Madhav Rao's greeting of "Hear the rain!" and "You are wet!" sounded like ebullient volleys of gunfire against the heraldic downpour. A colossal cloudburst dumped pelting hail on the roof and passed, leaving the audience exhilarated and expectant. Plants would swoon with the vibrations in here. Two rows in front of her Anna saw a feather that had once been pink and straight, and next to Lulu Croft's monsoon-hit headgear, her husband's head and shoulders. She couldn't tell whether the speeches conformed to Sir Basu's oratorical standards. Most were not in English and the others might as well not have been. But reliable old formulas like boycott, militant struggle, and Home Rule flew like sparks from the podium, catching fire as the audience echoed and applauded them. The news that someone had died a sudden death was received with broad smiles and cheers. Anna was certain, and said so at her dining table in Sussex soon after the war, that the meeting was prophetic. There were stupendous events to come. Her distinguished guest looked frankly skeptical. His wife remarked it was all very dramatic, but how could she possibly have come to such a conclusion when she didn't speak the language? And Anna, conscious of her husband's amused smile, said she had so often been at a loss in languages she knew, that she had had no trouble understanding one she didn't.

Henry, at least, understood exactly what she meant when

she described the scene to him the day after the meeting, though he called it the last of the old days, not the beginning of a new era. End or beginning made no difference. She and Henry got so carried away talking about the changes they were going to see during their lives, they forgot the time on a walk to a view Anna had never come across. The road above them led high up to frozen mountain passes. A spring broke into confusion at their feet, hurled itself over a precipice and shattered like glass on rocks below. They stood side by side, awed and elated, watching the light splinter its flying fragments long after their eyes had met in reluctant agreement that it was time to go. A tremendous future waited, he had promised. She could see it, the comradeship, the laughter, the abiding answer, once the agonies of the present had sorted themselves out.

Lulu Croft saw Anna as they left the meeting. "You should have sat with us, Miss Hansen. Marlowe could have translated for you."

"Hey, it's stopped raining," said Croft. "Why don't you come on back with us? We'll talk about it over supper and I'll see you home."

Anna had not been inside their house. Sir Basu's, supplied only with what he needed for a three-month stay, had no fancy extras, but his books and papers gave it an occupied air. The Crofts' was plainer and its whitewashed walls and cotton rugs were a far cry from Henry's wallpapered, painted and polished, stone-and-timber villa. She had not expected such stark differences between a mission and a Residence. The sweeper's child tiptoed in, his eyes on two covered china dishes rattling against each other on a metal tray.

"First time he's waited on table," Croft explained, "his new name is George Jeremiah. We call him Jerry."

A high laugh escaped Lulu.

"Marlowe's gone and baptized him."

"Now he can join the others in class and get an education without offending any sentiment. There was no other way to solve my dilemma."

"Your dilemma!" cried Lulu. "What about *his* dilemma?"

"At six years old nobody has what you could call a dilemma, Lulu."

"He's not going to be six years old all his life. What's going to happen to him when we leave?"

Croft bowed his head to say grace.

"I haven't thought about it," he admitted after grace. "I'll know what to do when the time comes. We could take him along with us."

"Who's we?"

"Frankly, Miss Hansen," he said, ignoring his wife, "I don't see us leaving. There's so much work right here. Building the church comes first and it's going to take time. But then there's this whole valley. No one has preached the gospel here before, or anything else. These hill people have no real religion. They worship nature spirits. I am incredibly fortunate to have the task of bringing them into the church laid upon me."

"And me," reminded Lulu.

"Mrs. Croft is right. We have so much to do we can't even think in terms of leaving."

George Jeremiah came in on his toes with one more dish and Anna shared the Crofts' baked beans and brown bread, with tinned Oxford sausages sent by the District Magistrate. A wooden bowl held pale gold apples from Stella's tree.

"How did you name him George Jeremiah, Mr. Croft?"

"Well, George for the King, I guess, and Jeremiah just came to me. I don't know why we shouldn't adopt him."

"Who is we?" Lulu's voice cracked, "If *you* do, Marlowe, I'm warning you I shall leave. Stella Brewster isn't the only one who can walk out. You don't know what you're talking about."

Croft gave his wife a long, steadying glance. "Calm yourself, Lulu. I'm not about to do anything right away, and we don't need to discuss this in front of Miss Hansen."

"There's a limit to greatness," said Lulu louder. "The world is how it is. Don't go on and on rearranging it."

"You'll have to excuse Mrs. Croft," said Croft regretfully. "She will come round to my point of view."

Two wars later Anna met indomitable conviction again when she and her husband, a Member of Parliament, were touring Central America, where it had been delivered to a village café no bigger than a Himapur tea shack in bottles, tins, and packets. They waited in the café where "It's the G.I. jive! Ma-a-an alive!" bounced out of a juke box while their car tire was being changed. A porter who had finished unloading Coca-Cola and pineapple chunks sat propped against a crate outside, fanning flies that clung like raisin clusters to his ancient face. Our common people, smiled the government guide, what a fine breed, the backbone of our economy. This old grandad, as you can see, is taking a well-deserved rest in the shade from the happy-go-lucky life the peasants lead, always singing and dancing. When they're not cheering the dictator's Cadillac on its way to the airport to negotiate more deals that will keep the economy in fine shape and the peasants singing and dancing, her husband had whispered. After that trip, indomitable conviction had had George Jeremiah at one end of it and a pineapple chunk on the other.

Anna could not ask Croft about the meeting until he was walking her home.

"Frankly I was disappointed," he confessed. "I went there hoping they would get down to brass tacks, and tackle the caste system, but not one man on the dais mentioned caste. They were worried about the way England is trying to weaken the Ottoman empire and Persia, and they were angry about England's transfrontier policy, like the invasion of Afghanistan in 1890. It's all part of the growing anti-European feeling since the Russo-Japanese War. And of course they want more say in government and higher ranks in the army opened to Indians."

Rain-laden branches sent rivulets sliding down their open umbrellas. Their rubber boots sank into clinging black mud. Until untouchability was rooted out, said Croft, fiery speeches would get them no nearer freedom. They had to cleanse themselves first. The sinner must repent of his own deeds. Yes sir. The meeting's sparkling, infectious, unintelligble rage drained out of Anna. She began to doubt she had seen a meteor cross the sky, and been riveted to her chair only a little while ago by words she did not understand.

"What the country needs, Miss Hansen, is a reforming zealot."

"There have been reforming zealots."

"Now that's interesting. Who?"

"The Buddha, for one."

Croft stopped to chuckle under a heavy branch and their umbrellas got a record drenching.

"I have to hand it to you. You Danes have an original sense of humor." He went into the adventures of the darning needle and other examples of sophisticated humor from Andersen's fairy tales that a vaguely Danish relation had introduced him to as a child. Who else would have thought of the darning needle feeling slimmer when she wore black? "But seriously, I find Mr. Brewster's attitude disappointing too. All he can say about untouchability is that he will not interfere. There is no proper religion around here to interfere with. Those men you heard tonight are high caste Hindus from the plains. The natives of this area have no religion."

"Me neither," murmured Anna in Danish.

"You were talking about indentured laborers the other night."

"Who were building the Uganda railroad?"

"I was thinking of the ones in South Africa. They've found a leader over there, a lawyer called Gandhi, who's got the right idea. He has organized the miners and led a very successful strike. Someone with the same businesslike strategy has to get to work on caste. Don't tell me it can't be done. Every problem has got a solution. It only has to be found."

"I see the light in the window of our house," said Anna. "So good night, Mr. Croft, and thank-you."

She remembered the dead man before she had gone far, and called out to Croft asking who had died.

"Pardon me, Miss Hansen? Oh, that was the meek and mild Indian, Kipling's caricature. They said he died in 1897. They said Tilak's first sedition trial put an end to that mentality. Maybe it did, but that's not the way I see it, not as long as they're caste-ridden. Tilak is a pretty sick man. Getting down to brass tacks will need health and vigor, plenty of get-up-and-go."

He went on his way, well pleased, Anna thought, with his prescription for a hefty successor to Tilak.

In 1961 Anna's grandson-in-law, who was working on a conference paper on Tilak's leadership of the Congress, said to his wife, "It's funny how your Gran felt a sort of kinship with him in spite of not meeting him."

Jason had brought Anna's letters to the kitchen table though he had finished work for the day.

Gayatri wore jeans to parties and floated around the kitchen of their London flat in saris and bangles. She had spent an hour stirring vermicelli in a quart of milk for his birthday dessert, an aspect of wifely devotion borrowed for special occasions from her Danish and English relatives. Otherwise she had inherited her strong-minded mother's strong Indian genes and political involvement. Her long-lashed eyes and long, romantic hair screened (for the first minute and a half of acquaintance) the toughest independence Jason had ever encountered. Anna had told him Gayatri needed a serene, nonviolent nature like his to settle down with. She said she knew from her own father's experience that changing the world was an exhausting business. Revolution had no off-season. Only the right life partner could ease the burden. The marriage could not have been more satisfactory if Anna had arranged it herself, which in a way she had.

"Gran didn't meet anyone politically important," said Gayatri, stirring endlessly, with a patience Jason had associated with Indians until he met some and discovered they couldn't even stand in a queue. "Remember, there was no mixing except with stooge Indians. I told you she worked for one of them. Gran said he believed in the slow, majestic forces of progress under the grand and glorious British. I would have laughed myself into a coma if I'd been there."

"No, you wouldn't." Jason sorted through the packet of letters Anna had sent him when he had written asking her for atmosphere. "You would have been progressing slowly and majestically yourself like all good nationalists. Tilak became the odd man out. The curious thing is Gran becoming so fascinated by someone she never saw. Here's the letter I was looking for." He read it to her:

Dearest Nicholas—I was deeply moved by the meeting for Tilak. There must be something extraordinary about a man who can set even these woods ablaze, so far from Delhi, and after so many years' absence. It must be unbelievable for him to be out of solitary confinement, to be able to walk about in open space, talk to other people, laugh out loud, and at night to look up at the stars and their companions and know he is free at last! After the silence of bricks and stones, one upon another making a prison, how wonderful it must be to hear real silence. He is back among his own people but it is a sad homecoming. His wife died while he was in jail. I suppose for such people life does not have much to do with happiness. But to make up for his personal loss, his national family has grown enormously. He has had a hero's welcome on his return. The judge who condemned him as a common criminal (and the stupid English on the jury) must be wicked or mad. I sat at the meeting Nicholas, understanding not a word, yet understanding it all, so vividly could I see the spoken passion of these people taking other forms in days to come, though the rain and hail were as deafening as the charge of several light brigades on the roof.

"That's a kind of document all by itself," said Jason.
"And typically Gran. But she wasn't anywhere near politics. First she was in a sort of ashram. Then she wandered around Calcutta, and her entire stay in Himapur, which

got cut short by the war, was spent between the stooge's house and borrowing books from the Residence."

Gran was unique and had been a marvel in her time, but it hadn't been a very interesting time. Tilak had just come out of jail, the rest of them had been slowly passing glorious resolutions while he was behind bars, and nothing like a real national movement had got started. There hadn't been the ghost of a peasant or a worker on the political horizon until later. Jason should have taken a livelier period, 1920 on.

"The point is," said Jason, "nothing would have turned out as it did afterwards if these particular things hadn't happened before—the stooge being a stooge, the D.M. lending your Gran books and pining for his wife, and the rain coming down in torrents over it all."

Gayatri turned off the flame and joined him at the table.

"Even Tilak, after all his talk of freedom, made recruitment speeches and asked Indians to rally round the British flag when the war broke out. I was never so disillusioned in my life," she said, as if she had been there, fully recovered from her coma.

"He said he'd join up himself if his age didn't disqualify him. It electrified a public meeting. Eight hundred and fifty young men volunteered on the spot."

"The government must have been thrilled to bits."

"By that call to arms? They banned his speech making at once. They weren't taking any chances."

But Esteemed had outfoxed them by sitting mum on the platform at public meetings, and letting other speakers deliver his thundering messages for him. Tilak, in fact, was Jason's bond with Anna. He had met her at a tiny function to commemorate a Tilak anniversary. She had invited him to lunch, introduced him to Gayatri not long after, and talked to him about Himapur for hours, leaving him with riddles that never seemed to get solved, perhaps because of the mist and the rain. She had said facts as plain as day had dimmed, blurred, and disappeared before her very eyes. Impossibly fantastic things had seemed to happen. Absence had been easier to grasp than presence. And the only thing that had never let her down through it all was a queer current of kinship. She had felt an inexplicable affection for people she had met just once or twice, and for some she had not met at all.

Anna was unique, Jason and Gayatri agreed. They dissected her remarkable personality and put it together again while the birthday vermicelli called *kheer* cooled. Gayatri got up to decorate it with slivered pistachios and a layer of silver leaf from a Delhi bazaar, and put it into the fridge for tomorrow.

The cook and George Jeremiah had gone to their quarters when Marlowe arrived home. Lulu was still up. She was so aghast that George Jeremiah might join the family, she had not remembered to take herself to bed. She started nervously in her chair at the sight of Marlowe in the entrance, filling the doorframe, without a squeak of his gum boots or a sound of his heavy, deliberate tread on the bare wooden boards of the veranda. With his hair plastered down he looked like a huge, wet dog.

"Where on earth have you been, Marlowe? It's a good hour and a half since you left with Miss Hansen." Lulu listened to her brittle voice as she would have to a strange, ungovernable sound outside herself.

Marlowe had left his umbrella on the veranda. He took his raincoat off, shook it, and hung it up by its loop on a metal hook behind the door.

"I took a walk to the churchsite, Lulu."

"At this time of night?" her voice rose, "and in this weather? Whatever for?"

Marlowe stood in the middle of the living room rubbing his palms together.

"I wanted to get some idea of how the rain had affected it."

"Couldn't you wait till morning?"

"Some of the land around here is not as solid as it looks. I wouldn't want the church washed away in the first monsoon after it's built."

It was useless trying to convince Marlowe there would be no church. She was neither for nor against the church because there wasn't going to be one. Marlowe was behaving like a crazed Bedouin chasing mirages of flashing water in the desert. She got up without another word and went to the bedroom.

"The site is pretty well flooded, as I expected," said Marlowe, coming in.

Lulu undressed and went to bed.

"I didn't like the look of it at all. I will have to hunt around for a more suitable site. Lulu," he said puzzled, "you didn't say your prayers."

"No, I didn't, did I? Well you can say them for me."

In the dark he seemed to be all over the room, a shaggy, shapeless force that did not fumble, hesitate, or bump into anything. He had never been dependent on her in any vital sense but not till tonight had she understood his complete autonomy. Marlowe had married her but not for love. There in the church it was she who had dedicated her whole soul to him and his work, though not, she could now see, for love. Love was what Henry Brewster had for Stella. Lulu had only been a good wife. With her good wifeliness gone, and her loyalty to his loyalties at breaking point, what was left for Marlowe to like about her? The life she had made with him was over. She had to think of herself. She could do it now that Marlowe's spell had worn off. Until this evening Lulu had not realized how like a sadhu's hypnotic spell it had been. Her ayah had once told her a bedtime story about a sadhu with tantric powers who wanted a young woman, and, when she refused to go to him, had asked her for a lock of her hair. She had cut the fringe of a carpet and sent it to him instead, and in the middle of the night, said the ayah, the carpet got up. It twisted and curled and lashed about like a snake under its trainer's command. It rose and fell like human breath. Then in dumb submission to the sadhu's will, it undulated through the sleeping city to his hermitage. Night after night the story retold itself. The eerie, petrifying vision curled and uncurled outside Lulu's mosquito net. No other story wiped it out. Lulu never dared ask her ayah what the sadhu did after he reduced the carpet to ashes with a burning, wrathful glance. She was thoroughly awake when Marlowe came out of the bathroom. She watched him kneel in prayer, get into bed, lie on his back, and pull up the covers to his chin.

Lulu's heart beat uncomfortably. She couldn't tell by his breathing whether he was asleep, or listening. Should she stay if he had second thoughts about George Jeremiah? But Marlowe never had second thoughts. Sometimes he put his first thoughts away until he could pull them out again. And George Jeremiah was only part of the problem. Lulu consoled herself with the prospect of leaving it all behind her. She had not meant it when she said she would, but now the idea seemed familiar, something she had been thinking about for a long time. She turned it around in her mind as she drifted toward sleep.

She was jerked wide awake. Marlowe lay like a log,

breathing, but not necessarily as if he were asleep. She had been a fool to imagine she could leave Himapur. She had never made a plan in her life or taken a journey alone, and Himapur must be the world's hardest place to leave. It was like discovering she was a cripple.

She remembered every jolting mile of the hilly journey up. It had invigorated Marlowe and depleted her. Where were they *going*, and why, when there was Calcutta to preach in? Her links with the hot, flat landscape of the plains grew remoter by the hour, and after their party of pack ponies and a tonga entered the forest belt, every known link snapped abruptly when she discovered—or had she been told earlier but never registered the fact?—that Marlowe had no church affiliation. His church had disowned him, or he it, after his arrest. He had no backing and was accountable to no one. They were heading for a backwater with no one financing the expedition or caring if they never came back. She fell asleep and dreamed of the journey down, down, into the valley below. Two coolies carried Lulu's dandy. It lurched from side to side on its pole like a raft on a choppy circular sea. The road went round in a circle. Long-necked, long-legged birds wheeled and dangled in a sprawling sky. Mountains squatted. There wasn't a soul in sight. She was giddy and nauseous when she opened her eyes. Marlowe's bed was empty. She could hear the faint scrape and rasp of his saw in the shed through the roar of tap water pounding into a brass bucket in the kitchen, to be heated over a wood fire for baths. She got unsteadily to her feet.

It was Saturday. After breakfast she sat with the sun on her feet and ankles, darning Marlowe's socks. By the time she had rolled them up and put them into her sewing basket, she could smile inwardly, superiorly, at her nonsensical fears. People left Himapur every day. Mail runners arrived. So did furniture, books, medicine, and a piano. She made up her mind to go to her parents without giving them advance warning. Her father's tigerish temper would have aged. They would take her back to England with them. She told Marlowe she was going up to the mall. The fresh air made her feel better and there was a bustle of shoppers at the chemist's. The shopman had his glasses on and couldn't see much through them, but in any case he had no manners. She had once heard him advise a colleague at the top of his voice, "Go report it to Brewster." When he had finished with his other customers he wasted the next two minutes putting bottles back on their shelves, then came along the counter in a leisurely way.

"Any medicine?" he inquired, without Good Morning or Madam or a smile.

Lulu withdrew the smile she had been about to grant him in view of the help she needed.

"Actually, I wanted some information."

Silence.

"How long does it take one of your consignments to get here?"

He stared at her, uncomprehending.

"You know," she said impatiently, "your pills and things. Boxes and crates." She was aware it sounded foolish, but those who had no training in planning, and didn't want their plans known yet, had to proceed clumsily.

"From the rail station? Eight or nine days on muleback."

Well, I'm not crates and boxes, she thought, but I'll be in a dandy and the coolies will be resting at the drop of a hat if I know them.

"How long did it take Mrs. Brewster—for example, and her luggage, of course, to go down?"

"Down? To what place? To the rail station, or Lucknow or what?"

"To the first resthouse to begin with."

Madhav Rao frowned and said how was he to know, but the coolies who had gone with the luggage were in the rickshaw shed. If she wanted, he could ask them. He didn't look very obliging, and, glancing over to the shed where the coolies sat curtained by heavy blue smoke, all turning to look at her through it, she hastily declined the offer.

"You see," she said, "Mr. Croft and I are thinking of taking a trip."

Madhav Rao asked sharply, "Now? You are closing the school and going down?"

Lulu rectified her blunder. "No, no, of course not. I'm talking about much later, during the holidays," leaving him looking as perplexed. "It's nothing. You can forget I spoke to you."

With all the fuss he'd made about Christian Endeavor, anyone would think he'd be delighted if the school closed.

"Any medicine?" asked Madhav Rao again as another customer entered the shop, and moved away when she said no.

Lulu wandered over to the ridge. The lifeless panorama on the other side had nothing growing on it but dead, grey grass and thorn bushes. The rocks were dry and wrinkled. Even a goat would think twice about attempting tracks faint as scars on that side. Nothing human could possibly come and go. Under the midday sun quartz glittered like powdered crystal on the denuded hills.

On Monday she saw how foolish she had been, wracking her brains about how to leave. She knew what she had to do when the Hansen creature started sun saluting. Lulu talked to her hurriedly after the exercise class, keeping one eye on the woodshed. She needed a travel escort, she said, and Miss Hansen must understand the request was confidential for the time being. T. H. rolled down her sleeves, gave her a searching look and asked if she really meant to leave. As Lulu watched her walk away she took the first deep breath she had taken in years. She would tell Marlowe at the right time. Days later the right time had not come and Lulu had a sickening certainty she would never leave.

◇

In the glade along the shortcut the postmaster called "dark," berry bushes turned bronze when late afternoon sunlight slanted through the pines. The hour of bronze was solid and enduring, and the glade had an eternal presentness the rest of Himapur lacked. With a slight shudder the hills could shrug off light encumbrances. Soil slipped under rain. A few minutes' drizzle blotted out human footprints and animal tracks. A storm like the other night whipped bushes to the ground and wrenched small plants from their moorings, leaving gaping holes where they had been. But visiting showers refilled the holes, and winds somersaulted the debris and deposited it on high or low land as if an army of cleaners had gone to work. Anna noticed the storm had affected the glade, too. Uprooted nettles and fallen branches sprang surprises on her path. She could no longer rely on a haven here in the glade. She spread her cardigan on the pine-needle floor and sat down.

"The trouble with your father is," Aunt Inge had written, with the mixture of exasperation and indulgence that the family had for Johannes, "he is always making personal decisions into policy decisions. I said to him, if you don't like goat's cheese, then you don't like it, and it is an end of the matter. But not for Johannes. He must like or dislike it depending on the life story and mating habits of the goat, and the satisfactions of the he-goat and the she-goat in the relationship. He must also go into the long grass or the short grass of their background, and concern himself with the goals and anemia of the cheese makers. At least it certainly sounded like it till finally your mother said, For goodness' sake, Johannes, just say yes or no. Do you or don't you want some of this cheese?"

Only, thought Anna, why was answering yes or no supposed to be such a trifle? One-word answers were the tips of icebergs. Nicholas knew it. She took his letter out of her pocket. He had not asked her a single question. He had not even hinted it was time to make up her mind. It was a cool, analytical letter about negotiations that were failing because secret treaties and rivalries canceled open appeals. Europe, he wrote, was on the brink of war. But how could it be? No other letter from home said so. How could thrones and countries bound by blood and culture tear up thirty years of peace because some one had shot an archduke, was how Aunt Inge had put it in hers. The whole idea was ridiculous to Aunt Inge, in her unimportant little country, but not apparently to the Great Powers who had their greatness and power to preserve. And it seemed there was not an inch of the earth's surface, not a railroad or a sea route or a market, that was not absolutely indispensable to some European nation's greatness and power. But Nicholas wasn't seeing the conflict, if it came, in terms of power or paranoia. Anna was poignantly aware of his lonely vigil at his desk at the Foreign Office, as he waited for his beloved Europe to plunge a knife treacherously into her own vitals. The breakdown of European concert was not only the end of peace. It was a threat to civilization.

She could hear him saying all that he had left unsaid. Far be it from him to advise or interfere, but if she had finished following in the footsteps of Hieuen Tsang and sundry other pilgrims before and after the seventh Christian century, sanity decreed she turn westward before the seas became impassable. With all the emotional extravagance she could spend on a pea, had she none to spare for the calamity facing a world in which the west would be at war with itself? His letter ended: "As I have watched the situation slip out of control, I've had the feeling we are losing control of our own lives as well. Private matters will soon be at the mercy of bigger outer events, for that, ultimately, is the tragedy of war. It is a fearsome thought. No modern European can ever have felt so helpless." It conveyed a sense of doom too vast for tears, yet tears rose to her eyes, for Nicholas, deprived of his shining confidence in life and progress.

She had gone to see her picture yesterday, and Madhav, with a shrewd glance at her face, had made his own diagnosis.

"The world changes, Tantanna, when our perception of it changes."

Why shouldn't he believe it? Millions of people did. The remedy lay in bringing life into proper focus, and Lo, all things could be borne. He instructed the lantern-lit room in the labyrinth at the end of the passage to put extra milk and sugar in her tea for her temporary revival.

Tea came. They drank it out of polished brass tumblers engraved Madhav Rao & Son in the brooding presence of The Camera. He explained, this time with a jeweler's precision, how the dissolution and creation of the cosmos were acts within one's reach—after long and diligent practice naturally, and only if one wanted Realization more ardently than anything else. Success was the result of years of physical and mental exercises and a loving nature, though love could get you there quicker than exercise, as in his father's case, before Madhav reached puberty. The end of the quest was astoundingly simple. You could see what you had not been able to see, though it had been there all the time. In that altering cosmic second the world around you vanished, and calm eternal beauty took its place. Travelers from many lands had described it. His father's experience had transformed the PWD building in Bombay and made it wondrously shimmering to behold. In Reality it had an amazing radiance. He had opened his eyes to a world transcending turmoil, suffering, and decay.

"It is within your reach, Tantanna, if you can jump over your mind."

"Why don't you jump over yours?"

"How are you telling me to jump over mine knowing very well I must educate my sons, get them wives, and see them in government jobs? Do you think I am my father? I am an ordinary fellow. It is different for you. Before marriage ladies have nothing to do."

"I am also not your father," she pointed out, and yearned for speedy salvation. "I have no great deeds stored up from my past lives to make my jump easy."

"Have I once told you it is anything to do with great deeds?"

Tza, he said, it was small deeds, sweetness, kindness. When his father was born, a sage told his grandmother she had given birth to a son who in his previous life had been a mahatma. When his previous parents died in the bubonic plague, he brought up his sisters tenderly, arranged good marriages for them, mended crows' wings, helped cows to calve. When he died he was mahatma to the whole village.

Madhav was satisfied with her portrait, a severely balanced composition in which she and the tree had equal status. And seeing that she was in such low spirits, he had not expected any comment from her.

The damp earth gave no warning of approach. Marlowe

Croft, no one's idea of an ethereal sprite, materialized out of thin mountain air. She was stupidly slow to react and he begged her pardon for startling her.

"I almost turned around and went back," he said. "You were so lost in thought, I hated to intrude."

"Oh please. It is not my property."

"It's a great little site, well protected from the seasons. After I left you home the other night I went to take a look at the upper level I had my eye on for the church. It won't work."

"It is my opinion you will need a mobile church for this area, Mr. Croft. Then you could wheel it about avoiding the weather. And if things become, as you say, rough, up here, you can roll it all the way down to the plains with no damage."

Croft gave her a keen look and burst into entirely boyish laughter. "You may have something there, Miss Hansen. You Danes, what a sense of humor. Do you mind if I join you for a few minutes?"

He sat down on a tree stump.

"This site is not ideal, but it is about the most reliable one I've seen. I'm going to ask the District Magistrate if he will release it. I hate to keep bothering him when he has problems of his own. He must be a sad man these days. I guess Mrs. Brewster didn't have his stamina for this kind of life."

"You must have met her."

"We met a few times. A lovely lady."

Anna waited, curiously tense, for him to go on, but Croft said, "I am more and more convinced there is no hope except Christian teaching up here. What else can wipe out the caste system?"

"Henry Brewster says caste and hierarchy are in their blood. Only their own people can tackle them."

Plans for Departure

"Now that's where I find him so defeatist. But it's a challenge, I grant you that," admitted Croft gloomily, sunk in thought on the tree stump.

Anna found Sir Basu ambling about the garden, as he called the overgrown grass in front of the cottage, droning the only song he knew under his breath. She had assumed from its sliding notes and little trills that it was a Bengali folk ditty until she listened to the words one day: "Don't get excited, don't get misled. Matilda went home with a pain in her head." His nose pointed grassward, his eyes were on his tennis shoes. He looked small and baggy. He lifted a vague hand in greeting and dropped it as he ambled past her. All wrapped up in the mimosa's hangover or the carrot's nervous breakdown, Anna thought. This bit of ground could have been on its way to becoming a garden if he had shown any interest in it.

"We will clear this and plant a little border?" she had asked hopefully, surveying the weedy, neglected patch the day after her arrival.

He had been positively alarmed. "Whatever for? I am renting this house only for three months."

"But we will enjoy it while we are here, and someone else is sure to come after us."

Looking like a grumpy Pompeiian in flight from Vesuvian lava, he had said before fleeing indoors, "Do what you like, Miss Hansen. But you must understand I have no time for anything superfluous. My Work will not brook interruption. I have come here to plan my Work."

Didi had told Anna he greatly admired the European mania for establishing institutions that would outlast them, but apparently it did not apply to a scraggy plot he would never see again after August. Didi had also warned her he was mortally afraid of interruption. "You can ask Potla for his life's savings and he will gladly give them to you, but do not ask him for his time, Anna. He will get into a panic, poor Potla."

Disregarding Didi's advice, Anna had coaxed and schemed in her early days to whisk him off on walks and help him track down rare finds, while as an added bonus they would discover gorgeous views and picnic nooks where they would eat light fruit lunches.

"There must be places from where you can see the best views."

"There is a place called Dorothy's Seat in Naini Tal," he said dreamily, the first time he had thought about it in forty-two years, he told her.

"Who knows, Dorothy could be having a seat here," she said, encouraged by his tone, but he said he had never heard of one, and that he had just been reminded of the purest profile he had ever seen. He had shared Dorothy's Seat with the profile for perhaps two seconds before its possessor had joined her family at the telescope to look at the view.

The dry, gray grass had grown thick, poky, and beyond reform when the rains began, but Anna had persuaded Henry's gardener to bring over potted plants to beautify the veranda, wire baskets of geraniums to hang along it from among the dozens he had in his nursery, and a tub with a rose tree, all returnable after three months.

Sir Basu was ambling toward her again. This time he stopped and remarked she was not looking herself at all, and hoped she was not coming down with a cold.

The next day, Anna woke tired and tormented with indecision. She got out of bed, put on her dressing gown and slippers, and went out to the front veranda. She had never been up so early. Sir Basu sat in the pallid sunshine, reading a week-old newspaper, his tea tray beside him. It would be another hour before the cook brought her tray to her room.

He studied her critically and again hoped she was not coming down with a cold. Colds were catching. He noticed she was wearing a gown resembling a Japanese kimono, made of fluffy blue material he would not have expected a practical woman to choose. It had unnecessarily long hanging sleeves and no sign of a pocket. It reminded him of his sillier nieces. What needed keeping warm, her feet, were as bare as nature had made them, in skimpy slippers. Odd, considering she had knitted socks for him, the cook, and the coolie who brought the firewood. Fortunately they were not identical. His had a pattern, theirs were plain.

"Now you are here, you might as well tell the cook to bring you a cup."

It was not a very cordial invitation, but the cold or bronchitis she was coming in for had made her listless. Obediently she drifted indoors. Her company at morning tea did not class as an interruption, but it was an intimate rite he had shared with no other human being since Didi's children had been children and swarmed all over him like savages on his rare visits to the family. Miss Hansen came back with a cup. He wondered if she always looked subdued at this hour. For all her adventures in the sun her face was alabaster smooth and her hair had the innocence of fresh butter. Ageless Miss Hansen, it dawned on him, had an age, and it was young. Didi had sent a young woman, a European, all this way, alone, without advice about hats, flannel underwear, and numerous other matters that Europeans should be informed about. The revelation so unnerved him he dismissed the Balkans from his mind. In any case, far worse than he was reading about in the newspapers must have happened by now. Only Henry Brewster would have the latest news. As to Miss Hansen's sincerity and courage, why, but for these, would she have come? Didi's rash irresponsibility made him feel doubly and urgently responsible.

"Do you hear from your parents?" he asked.

"My *parents*?"

"Your parents."

"Of course I hear, also from my brothers and my aunt. They are all in Denmark."

"Then what are you doing here?"

To his dismay she wiped her eyes on one of her unnecessarily long sleeves.

"I meant nothing personal," he quickly assured her, and added earnestly, "your presence here has been the greatest help to me, Miss Hansen."

"I wish you would call me Anna," she said with a small catch in her voice and relapsed into such a doleful silence he was sure she was ill, though he agreed at once to call her Anna.

"You must let me have your father's address. I should have written to him much before this to tell him you are all right."

"He already knows it from my letters."

"Nevertheless," said Sir Nitin firmly.

Miss Hansen's Japanese sleeves, long as they were, could no longer cope with her tears and she made no attempt to conceal them. Sir Nitin was gravely disturbed. He had seldom seen anyone so overwrought so early in the morning. He would have done anything in his power to help her. Inwardly he debated suggesting a short walk on level ground later in the day if that would cheer her up, and perhaps he should ask her to call him uncle. It would have helped to know what the matter was, but quite properly she kept her troubles to herself and said, no thank-you, she did not need a doctor. It was nothing to do with her health. Being conscientious, she got down to work as usual after breakfast and she was much better by afternoon, though far from normal. Instead of striding off on a six-mile walk or paying a visit to Brewster's library to look into the dead past, she sat in the back yard with a book she did not read. Sir Nitin could hardly bear it and he pottered about the house keeping a discreet eye on her. Once or twice he went to the veranda and smelled a rose. It could be homesickness, quite understandable in a woman so far from her parents, her brothers, and her aunt. In that case, he supposed, it would not be long before she was restored to the bosom of her family.

He pottered into the dining room humming Matilda, and sat down at the table with no aim or object in mind on this idle, structureless afternoon. A peaceful quarter hour enfolded him in its tent of soft satin. Other times of his life, opinions he had formed and held, and forgotten why, returned to keep him company. He was young, with a round, winsome face. He called "Shot!" and "Point!" gaily on the tennis court and drank port-and-lemonade after the game. Mr. Gladstone was as near a household god as a reformed household would allow. His picture had a place of honor in the hall. Progress was in the air, and a new intelligentsia brimful of a new education walked in and out of Nitin's father's house. There was nothing tomorrow would not bring. I am partial to the doctrine of enthusiasm, a sonorous Indian voice declared from a public platform. Never before, not in the most celebrated Hindu reign or even in the empire of the great Akbar, had Indians spoken as one nation, said another. There had been no time like this.

Oratory knew no bounds. The Indian princes were England's allies, the Indian people were her freeborn equal subjects under the Crown. Solemn charters and statutes guaranteed it. In this ideal, intoxicating relationship the sovereign showed love, care, and sympathy for India, and Indian hearts beat with devotion to the British throne. Enfranchisement and autonomy were around the corner. India's sons would soon sit in the councils of Empire to govern and guard it as perfect equals. The grand Gladstone had understood the terms of the pact when he said that England's power in India rested on the will of two-hundred-and-forty-million Indians.

Nitin's youth was so filled with the music of the future, he had not noticed when the music stopped. The white man invented a burden in its place, and jingles to go with it that drowned out Gladstonian chords. Promises and pledges became pieces of wastepaper. It was the most moderate of moderates who had finally cried out in anguish, "Let them fling their promises into the flames. Let them tell us once and for all that we are a conquered people, and have no rights and privileges." The words probed unbearable hurts and humiliations. Natural science had kept him quarantined from these too. He had been the only Indian invited to the select dinner for Robert Pryor, new Home Secretary to the government of the province.

Nitin spent the years of national protest against the partition of Bengal in his laboratory, while the fanatics seized arms and ammunition from wherever they could and took to revolutionary violence, and Bengal's greatest poet marched across Calcutta at the head of a procession, singing a song he had composed for the occasion. Art, of course, was different from science. Mathematics, journalism, scholarship were all very different from science. The immunity of science was pierced only once, on a sultry night in Allahabad by a chant he knew in his bones must be Tagore's song on the move. His students, scientists all, were singing it. They passed under his window with candles, went around the building and down the road. Surrounded by specimens in glass cabinets, he thought he heard the song retreat, but he walked down the stone steps of the building expecting to confront it, them, at the bottom and everywhere on the campus for months afterward.

"Sir Nitin?"

The dining room, unoccupied by either of them at this time on any ordinary day, had both of them in it, and he was so taken aback at Miss Hansen having mastered the correct form that he decided not to proceed with uncle.

"Have you decided about Mrs. Croft?" she enquired.

"It is not for me to decide. If she wants to travel with us, I can't prevent her. But it will be awkward without her husband's knowledge and approval."

Anna stifled an impatient retort. "She is going to speak to him."

"Well he is not likely to send her off with his blessing, is he? It is extremely awkward, being mixed up in a family quarrel."

With husbandleaving such an obstacle race, no wonder Stella had been smart enough to leave on a holiday. There had been no wrangle beforehand about breaking up a marriage to disturb the flawless arrangements for her departure. But Lulu had nowhere to go on a holiday. And being the inveterate bungler she was, she would bungle it and never get permission to leave at all.

Sir Nitin jumped up, guilty and alarmed at the passage of uncounted hours without a thought about his work, and went to his desk. Following his example, Miss Hansen also reverted to activity, but instead of a walk, she chose to circle the house like a marionette on wheels, propelled past his window every few minutes in a dizzying manner that gave him no chance to concentrate.

Anna heard a shrieking flurry die down to a croak as the cook wrung a chicken's neck. She quickened her pace in the opposite direction and sat down on a low stone parapet behind the house. Darkness drifted up from the narrow road below. Conclusions fell quietly into place. Strangely, the somber shadows of Nicholas's letter now illumined quite another world, one that would come into being as soon as enough people wanted it. At some time not far ahead, countries must shrink into Danish unimportance and languages be understood by inspired instinct. The woes of the Great Powers left her unmoved. She would have stayed on in Himapur even if she had had no personal reason, but, in fact, her personal and policy reasons were so joined, it was impossible to divide them.

T W E L V E

I t should have been relatively easy, with the wealth of classical and historical precedent of men who had spent years away from home, seeking fame and fortune, conquering this and that, to explain to Nicholas why a woman, for a change, could decide without guilt to extend her purely personal stay abroad. But it was proving extremely difficult. Anna wondered if it was because Nicholas's most cherished values had their permanent home in castles in the air. He belonged to a breed that had simply imagined a constitution and traditions into being. What really rhymed in his universe was breathed in and out. It never needed to be written or said. Something was wrong if explanation about a fundamental matter was necessary. And no language had yet been devised to tell a man you sincerely loved that you had met another extraordinary man whom you were dangerously close to loving.

"Anna, Anna!" Sir Nitin came agitatedly into her room. "Something terrible has happened."

He gave her a note Croft's carpenter had brought, asking her to come at once. The message was brusque. Mrs. Croft had been killed in an accident.

Anna found Croft standing hunched over the dining table, his hands resting squarely on it, his head bowed. The cook and George Jeremiah hovered half in, half out of the doorway. They huddled together to let her pass, but she stopped involuntarily on the lintel. When Croft straightened he stared through the trio, lifted his eyes to the ceiling, and launched into a wailing prayer, oblivious of his audience of three. The room filled with racked emotion, but Croft, Anna realized, was talking to himself. It was a funeral oration in praise of "this wonderful woman" that the actual funeral would not match, with an unconverted hillside dwarfing the ceremony at poor, unloved Lulu's grave. In the lull after his third Amen, Anna said uncertainly, "Mr. Croft? You sent for me?"

Croft stirred and the doorway emptied. Anna followed him into the bedroom in trepidation, but Lulu, dead some hours, and turning faintly mauve, looked more pathetic than frightening. She had a few cuts and bruises that aroused Anna's concern until she remembered Lulu was dead. Her fatal fall had not otherwise disfigured her. Her injuries must have been internal. She lay fully clothed, with her eyebrows raised high in a frozen spasm of surprise above her closed lids. Anna had heard Madhav Rao once say, talking of reincarnation, that some faces looked old and malevolent at birth. By no means did all newborn babies have adorable baby faces. Apparently others could show surprise at death. Lulu had been caught unawares by a deceptively firm stretch of road above a ravine. The doctor sent by Henry arrived, and Anna helped him to prepare the body for burial.

She and Sir Nitin attended the funeral the following day with Henry and a dozen or so of the Crofts' acquaintances. There had never been a more depressingly dry-eyed funeral. No relative was present to watch Lulu's body lowered into her grave. Croft said her estranged parents would not have come even if it had been possible for them to make the trip in time. Anna's despondency deepened with every spadeful of soil shoveled over the coffin. She laid her own small, fragrant posy of violets at the graveside and turned away without saying good-by to Croft, who was seeing Sir Nitin and other mourners into their waiting conveyances. Several rickshaws had trundled downhill past her in a row, jingling their bells, when he caught up with her.

"I want to thank you for all your help, Miss Hansen. I know you and Sir Nitin are leaving soon, but I would appreciate it if you would come tomorrow as usual, and keep on with your exercise class until the very last day. I know it's a big favor to ask but the school will go right on."

Anna was unpleasantly jarred.

"Mrs. Croft would have wanted everything to go on as before," he assured her.

It was preposterous. Lulu with her hats and her proprieties would at the very least have wanted a day's decent mourning. Even Croft should have known better than to go right on. The school, the "church," and zealous reform could surely wait twenty-four hours in memory of his wife. But Lulu seemed to have slipped soundlessly through a gap, the gap had closed, and there was not a seam or crack to mark it. On the very day of her loveless burial Croft was making it hard to remember she had been here at all. Anna said she would let him know. He did not deserve to be told she was staying on. She felt reluctant to go home and get down to her delayed letter to Nicholas. She wished there had been some sign of spontaneous sadness at the funeral. It had been correct and unfeeling, the formal rites, nothing more. She found herself walking to the level below the original churchsite. Lulu had had her accident where the elusive path abruptly disappeared. Anna looked down the slippery hillside, thinking her own memorial thoughts of

Lulu up to her urgent, furtive plea. Anna knew this walk
well. A careless foot could easily slip here. Her own had.
But Lulu's could not have, because Lulu hated walking,
and no walk-hater would choose to come in this direction.
No more would a rickshaw. Anna had never seen wheel
ruts on this walk. There was scarcely a visible footpath.
Had hostile rickshaw pullers deliberately brought Lulu here?
She had talked so much about their hostility. She had sworn
they would see her at the bottom of a *khud* if they had the
chance, the sullen looks they gave her. Croft had not mentioned a rickshaw ride in connection with her death but he
may not have known. She may have intended to go on a
shopping trip to the mall, and the coolies had brought her
here instead. There had been no one to hear her cries for
help. Lulu had thrashed about like a netted fish on the hor-
rifying ride. The rickshaw had rolled or been pushed off the
edge, and her penetrating scream had fallen like an arrow
into the ravine to get lost among the massed deodars lining
it. If that had happened, four men might, with practiced
effort, have dragged the rickshaw up again, or down further
to the glade at the next level. They were used to superhu-
man performances.

How exactly had Lulu died? She had never asked Croft
the question because she had arrived to find him on a tidal
wave of prayer, though for anyone but him it had been an
odd time to be praying. He had been suitably funereal at
the funeral, but it was business as usual as soon as it was
over. "I'm going to speak to Marlowe, of course," Lulu had
said with a glance over her shoulder at the woodshed. Marlowe? Lulu's body had had no marks of a struggle. An
instant's light pressure could have snuffed her out. For
Marlowe it would have been easier than throttling a doll.
Mrs. Croft did not come round to my point of view, Anna

heard him gravely explain. But when she blocked out Marlowe, Madhav Rao took his place. Could he have performed a sober patriotic duty with a little homemade bomb,
which he would disown with a clear conscience like his
shop? I am not a murderer, Tantanna, this is not murder,
echoed with queer insistence through her brain.

Anna suspected she was reacting to delayed shock, having gone through her neighborly, helping motions calmly
enough. She turned back and found the postmaster's shortcut to the glade. If there had been a rickshaw accident, there
should be traces of it, and she could stop coddling at least
one of her morbid fantasies. Later she would get all the
facts from Marlowe.

It was the first time the glade had lived up to its bad
reputation. It was dull and overcast, and more cluttered
with drifting debris than two days ago. But it had no dis-
membered remnants of a rickshaw accident, not so much
as a scrap of cloth or metal. A dirty rag hanging loosely
over the tree stump Croft had sat on aroused her curiosity,
but it turned out to be the poor, flattened corpse of a wood-
land creature, picked up and flung about like other unac-
countables by the recent rainstorm or a landslide, one of
the sudden appearances and disappearances her walks had
accustomed her to. She bent over it for a closer look and
began to tremble uncontrollably. She had never enter-
tained this particular morbid fantasy. It had nothing to do
with life as she knew it. This could not be Stella's pretty
spaniel in a state of gentle decay. But there was no mistaking Juliet. Mud caked her brown and white markings. She
lay on her side, her dainty paws extended, with one bedrag-
gled aristocratic ear covering part of her well-bred face.

· · ·

Jason's birthday lunch was over. The *kheer* had been acclaimed and he had been congratulated on a wife who had spent an hour at the stove stirring it. Anna telephoned after the party and wished them both many happy returns of Jason's birthday. Her buoyant voice took a load off their minds. They seldom discussed it, but they shared an anxiety that Anna would die before they had come to terms with the idea that a large part of their lives would have to be lived without her. She had been more than usual in their thoughts because of Jason's conference paper and her Himapur letters.

"I couldn't possibly have kept quiet about finding the dog," said Gayatri, who had heard her grandmother speak of the incident.

Jason agreed. There was nothing reticent or inscrutable about Gayatri's Oriental half. A sieve made a better guardian of secrets. But, he reminded her, Anna had had no one to talk to.

"I'd forgotten. She didn't have a soul. If she *had* told the stooge, he would have advised her to forget it. It would have taken a much braver man to take some action. What a servile bunch the leading lights were. One of them said God Himself had stretched out his right hand and placed the Empress's crown on Victoria's head."

But Jason thought it routine rhetoric, regardless of century, given empires. The mystique surrounding Victoria was to be expected. He said the stooge was not the reason why Gran had not spoken. The real reason was more desperate. In Himapur law and order was Henry Brewster. Gran must have felt frighteningly isolated with that knowledge growing cold inside her.

. . .

Confusion and horror nailed Anna's feet to the moist earth near the tree stump. She could not walk away from the fetid corpse any more than she could explain its presence in the glade. To tell you the truth, dearest Nicholas, I feel a little afraid, she had written of other, less paralyzing fears. Paintings and pictures are evidence, she had also written. Now the forest had offered up evidence of its own, as definite as a coin or a seal, of authentic, crowded, bygone events. It could be proof of more treasures awaiting excavation. What buried treasure would the next landslide uncover? Blankness assailed her when she tried to think of Henry. His hair and his eyes were colorless, so was his skin, and how little she knew about him. How wrong too, the little postmaster had been about crime in these parts. He would continue to be wrong, saying it was only a dog, not so serious as a human loss. It must have run away from the Klekter memsahib's departing caravan, got lost, and been killed. After all, these were woods.

Anna sternly marshaled her thoughts to consider the woods theory. A dog stalked and killed by a panther would be an eaten dog, and these would be skeletal remains, not a whole, slightly decomposing carcass waiting to be exhumed by a blast and draped nonchalantly over a tree stump in a glade of evergreens. And the rest of the theory was wrong too. For a runaway dog, an Englishman's love-lavished spaniel, unique in Himapur, search parties would have scoured these woods until it was found. It could only mean one thing. The caravan of Stella's luggage had gone, and no one knew the dog had not gone with it. Cabin trunks appearing and reappearing on muleback at every hairpin bend in the mountainside are solid and verifiable proof of departure. All the way up on the mall tea drinkers and shoppers had had diminishing flashes of the descending mule train. Mrs. Brewster's bag-and-baggage departure was the talk of the town. Who could ask for more evidence that she and her dog had departed? Not until she was nearly home did Anna remember why she had gone to the glade, and that Lulu's death had taken place on the same hillside now blossoming with excavated evidence of past deeds.

Henry was with Sir Nitin in the living room. She heard his voice in time to control her instinctive recoil and rearrange her features, but she could not speed the circulation of her blood. He got up and came swiftly to her.

"How exhausted you look. You've had a trying day. And I'm afraid the news is bad. Austria has declared war on Serbia."

His eyes were brown-irised and black-pupiled, his hair a dense, graying brown. There was nothing colorless about the vigor of his voice either, or his stride forward to take her hand and grasp it in a grip like stone.

"What about England?" she forced herself to ask.

"It's probably a matter of days."

Before the posies on Lulu's grave had wilted, the outer world had exploded into other declarations of war, Germany's on France, England's on Germany, Germany's on Russia, and, as part of the British empire, India was automatically at war on the midnight of August 4, 1914. But it was still the night of Lulu's burial when Henry, gripping Anna's hand, said, "All this has been terribly upsetting for you. You look so tired I won't suggest your coming back with me now, but won't you come and dine tomorrow? Sir Nitin says it would be good for you."

Sir Nitin added his concern and agreement.

After Henry had gone he tried to persuade her to go to bed. "You look badly in need of a rest. The cook will bring a tray to your room."

Lulu's death, homesickness, European war, or fatigue would each have been a valid excuse for numb silence and retreat. But people who lived under the same roof owed each other honest explanations. Anna refused a tray in bed. In their mutual relationship murder had applied to the plant kingdom. She began haltingly with the spaniel, dreading the long implausible recital ahead of her. To her intense relief Sir Nitin responded with a sixth sense and went straight to the heart of the matter. Their talk through dinner had a sharp, clean clarity. She discovered that great scientific minds are intuitive, but being a scientist he cautioned her not to jump to conclusions. He also gave her useful information. Since the Ilbert Bill had been passed by the Indian Legislative Council in 1884—against rowdy opposition from European planters and businessmen—a European *could* be tried by a senior Indian magistrate outside the Presidency towns in cases involving death, but the accused could claim a jury of whom half would be European. And Europeans, Sir Nitin said dryly, could not be seen to fall out with each other without disastrous consequences to imperial prestige. He quoted from European scripture:

> By all ye cry or whisper
> By all ye leave or do,
> The silent sullen peoples
> Shall weigh your gods and you.

Anna did not know the quotation, but she recognized pain as deep and permanent as her own was fresh. For the first time since she had known him, Sir Nitin's English had a bitter, foreign sound.

"In the circumstances, what chance would justice have?"

he asked. "They will be twice as careful now to keep bad examples of European behavior out of sight. A sensational trial might turn public opinion against cooperation with the war effort."

The cook cleared the table, and they heard him splashing cold water over greasy plates in the pantry. They were still at the table after he had eaten and come in again to ask if he should lock up for the night, and they sat on when he went away to his quarters.

"Above all, Anna, what can a court do without solid evidence, even suppose that rarity, an independent English judge and jury, can be found?"

If there was no evidence but Juliet, then there was nothing to be done. Anna closed her aching eyes and pressed her fingers against her lids. When she opened them her face was white and appalled.

"Have we really been talking about Henry?"

So that was it. Unused compassion stirred Nitin Basu. Poor child, he thought, poor child. He searched his vast human inexperience for some way to help her. There was really only one course open to them.

"We must leave as soon as possible. In any case, my dear, it is time for you to go home."

Chic Parisien had come with the day's mail. Anna took it to her room. She lay down with it and turned the pages. It was actually a Viennese magazine, and it informed her Austrian styles were following Paris, St. Petersburg, and Chicago. Designers favored spontaneity and gaiety. Evening gowns were being pinned up on dressmakers' dummies instead of being cut out on a table. There were daring departures. The most outrageous was the V-neck. Staid, high, boned collars were out. So was the little waist. However, London evening gowns continued more formal. On the occasion of her daughter's presentation at court, Lady Margaret Mayhew had worn a gown of violet satin with a chrysanthemum pattern brocaded in silver and a train of the same material lined in white satin. The sleeves were of matching silk net. Sparkling stones decorated the neckline and long bands of them hung down to hiplevel. An illustration showed them hanging down. For daytime the brand new "tailormade," with its pleated tunic and short jacket was in vogue everywhere. Lulu would have been entranced with the flippant little toques women were wearing on their heads, and the kiss-curls on their cheeks, in the country that had declared war.

The magazine slipped from Anna's hands. She lay on her back stock-still in bed and saw Stella's spaniel behind her closed lids, Stella's luggage caravan leaving without it, and Stella herself under layers of clinging black soil, her floating hair trapped under a fierce monsoon-growth of shoots. Unless it was all an insane illusion and Stella was in London, favoring Viennese spontaneity of design, and approving of the frothy confection taking shape on her dresmaker's dummy.

An agitated Stella presided over her dinner with Henry the next evening. Anna was thankful she had her back to the pictures and could listen with some pretense at concentration as Henry talked about Sir Edward Grey's peace proposals falling on deaf ears. England would not be able to remain neutral as the King and government had hoped. The King, the government, the European crisis. The impersonal dregs of conversation. His priorities had been rather different. They went into the library after dinner where Henry insisted on pouring her a brandy.

"An unexpected outcome of Mrs. Croft's death may be that Croft will get his churchsite," he said.

Anna took a fiery swallow. It deadened innocent membrane, leavng her mind as feverish and active as ever.

"Whoever comes after me will succumb to Croft," said Henry. "Once you let a missionary in, you can't object to his preaching or building a church to preach in. Apart from my own views on churches, his main obstacle was his unfortunate wife. She couldn't make a friend to save her life. How ghastly that sounds now."

"Was it a rickshaw accident?" asked Anna.

"If it was, no rickshaw coolie has come forward to report it and all traces have been obliterated, which is unlikely so soon. No, I gather she was alone. Her body was discovered by Croft himself, hours afterwards, according to the doctor."

"So anyone could have done it."

Henry looked at her with interest. "How sinister you make it sound, Anna. Surely you're not serious. Do you believe someone killed her? She was universally disliked but you don't kill a person out of dislike."

"Why do you kill a person?"

"What a question! Sufficient motive, I suppose. I am hardly an expert on the subject."

"Are you not? You deal with it."

"When I have to, yes, which isn't too often. There's little crime to speak of in these parts. But tell me more about your theory."

Unfortunately, her theory contained an unmentionable dog. Peace in her private world, and, it seemed to her then, her whole future, hung on Stella's spaniel. It could not be wished away. Nor could the parade of evil images it conjured, the thousand terrible images of Henry she had not been able to erase by staring into the stationary hours all last night or through the tender, gliding daytime mist at the window all day today. No wonder Henry could not sleep either. She began to talk about Marlowe Croft to keep from betraying her own real anguish, and shrank from the quick, expectant light in Henry's eyes as he grasped the opening and said in some ways Croft would certainly fill the bill. He explored all the facets of possibility while Anna kept her word to Nitin Basu.

A part of her brain tried to consider Henry objectively. He was no worse than others who had sent men and women to the stake, the gallows, and to every conceivable torture, in the service of their kings and churches. It had never prevented them from going home with a hearty appetite for dinner and chatting about the day's affairs. If there were fine distinctions between one kind of murder and another, they were too subtle for her. She would never understand the heart and mind of an assassin, whatever his motive. She was deathly sick of the war's bloodletting before it had even begun, and she would never be free of the horror of her discovery in the glade.

The brandy acted at last to dull her nerves, and to her fascination Henry began to talk about Stella. A mob of stone-throwers would judge her guilty of cheap, wanton desertion, he said. No one should. It was a lie. Their differences had been political. Stella was a soldier's daughter and granddaughter and had been brought up on Mutiny legend and lore. She had been taught that those who mutinied knew what was coming to them when they took the rocky road to revolt, whether they were gladiators in B.C., or Jamaican slaves, or Irishmen, and most of all if they were soldiers. The Peshawar uprising of June 10, 1857, was one of her father's favorite after-dinner stories. It had been simple prudence, he said, to pick forty of the hundred-and-twenty prisoners taken, and blow them from cannons as an example to the rest. No one pretended it was civilized, but which ultimate deterrent was? Englishmen had to overcome their natural abhorrence to atrocity and get their own atrocity in first so that it would act as a deterrent. It wasn't original either. The Moghuls had blown prisoners from cannons, and Moghul punishment had a big revival after the Mutiny. Mutineers had been branded with red-hot irons, bayoneted in the face, burned alive, and shot in batches of ten pinioned together.

"We didn't invent any of it, Henry," the Colonel, a man of persuasive masculine charm, had said, "and it did allow for quick disposal of a vast number of prisoners."

In Stella's bedtime stories the sun of 1857 had set in splendor over the razing of rebel villages and risen again over mass executions on roads and riversides. A gracious moon had smiled down on the golden cross of the Christian church in Delhi which, by the grace of God, had escaped the infidel bullet holes riddling other important landmarks. It was necessary in all Eastern lands, among semibarbarous people, to establish fear and awe of the government.

"With that upbringing, what else could Stella believe?"

"I have not been able to understand what you had in common with her," said Anna dully.

"Nothing," said Henry. "She didn't even know what I meant by love, and we certainly did not have it in common. Love must be one of the most unequal dispensations on earth."

"Where is Stella's father now?"

"He died a year ago. It was a terrible blow to her. She adored him. Her mother died when she was born."

Henry finished his brandy and put his glass down on the table.

"I suppose I'm free to live another sort of life, now that there isn't much freedom to decide what to do, and no telling how much is left of life."

"You will be leaving?"

"I've been told if we declare war, the government will allow civilian officers to serve in the forces. If so, I shall join up. Well, at least it will give me a plan."

He stood up gaunt and tall, making it appear an act of resurrection. He took down her Copenhagen address, and on the walk home she heard him say across the gulf that now separated them, he hoped very much they would meet again after they both left Himapur. In spite of everything his words had the same clear, confident ring. Till yesterday she had believed it was the ring of transparent truth.

T H I R T E E N

The fearful questions had never been answered because she and Sir Nitin had left them unasked. Their deadweight sailed back to England with Anna. The voyage across a rough Red Sea carried its own load of suspended hysteria. There was not a single normal passenger on board. Patriotism made them uplifted, exalted versions of their ordinary selves. The captain's compliments and flowers, and other ship courtesies resembled graceful last flourishes on a liner that some said might shortly be camouflaged a dull gray and become a troop conveyer. Those who had had the privilege of fighting in previous wars were impatient for action, and a general excited anticipation did the declaration of war proud. An impromptu concert was held in defiance of the weather soon after they sailed. In a rocky grand finale the solid soprano, vowing Britons never never can be slaves, tilted to and fro like an embroidered pendulum in her dress of sequined crêpe-de-chine, along with the table and its bowl of wax petunias beside her. Powerless to clap, the audience held on to the arms of their slithering chairs and made do with hectic cheers.

It was smoother sailing after they left the Suez Canal and entered the Mediterranean. A sunlit trance descended on the voyage. Anna's cabin was the only place for her once she saw how futile it was to try to avoid long lines of hatted Lulus reclining lifeless in deck chairs, and burly Crofts who gripped the railings with their powerful hands and stared stolidly into the spray. Every angular stranger anxious to be left alone was Henry. With an effort of will she choked down her questions and suppressed the senseless urge to shout them hoarsely out to sea. If they could not be resolved, she should be allowed to cast them overboard and forget them. She should be able to stop agonizing over the Henrys on board, wondering whether they shunned society because they were guilty of crimes they had not actually committed, or because loneliness is the lot of those who are ahead of their times. That, too, was now an academic question. A week in the calm, blue Mediterranean and a mist drifted down the Himalayas to veil her memories of Himapur. Croft and Lulu faded to a ghostly muslin glimmer. They might have been creatures of her own concoction. A distorted Henry wrestled with his demons. But Stella parted the fog with her fingers and stepped out, tragic in her regal velvet gown, to travel with Anna. Now that she was gone, she had surfaced with a limpid, perishable beauty meant for love's gentler pastures. She stood in a deserted corner of the deck with a low risen moon shining through her, sea salt beading her hair and arms with its crystalline residue. Only two people Anna had known behaved reasonable and receded naturally during the voyage, Sir Nitin, to whom she was bound in a conspiracy of restraint, and Madhav Rao, who had called to say good-by at the head of the parent delegation, bearing garlands, a coconut, advice, and an enamel pillbox of Indian earth for Tantanna.

Nicholas was deeply altered by the year's separation, exhausting hours of work, and the failure of his government's labors to prevent war. Anna would never have believed it if anyone had told her she and Nicholas would have nothing more to say to each other for the first hour of their reunion than I hope you had no trouble on the voyage, How are things at the Foreign Office, and variations of You're looking absolutely worn out.

When he had done his duty as a host and seen her comfortably settled, Nicholas said politely, "Stay as long as you like, it's a big house. I'll see what I can do about getting you a booking home, but it may take a long time."

It gave her a nasty shock. At the back of her mind, however far back, she had taken it for granted her travels had ended. She realized she would have to say so. Their mutual sensitivity was rusty with disuse. Nicholas was not a mind reader either, and his mind was heavily burdened by problems not remotely personal.

"I had thought of staying on in London," she said, equally polite and formal.

"Oh? Good. Then that's all right. Stay here as long as you like, unless you'd rather not, of course. What do you plan to do with yourself?"

Anna, who had not anticipated staying anywhere else, said she didn't know. Some work. War work, she supposed, since all work would be war work.

"I'm sorry I can't lunch with you on your first day back. I don't come home for lunch and I don't get back till late in the evening. A friend of my uncle's is coming to dinner tonight."

He left for his office and she for the guest room that recalled, as soon as she entered it, the grace and continuity of Nicholas's private world. There were things worth preserving and he had preserved them. A serene, intuitive order prevailed. It flowed out into the street and returned reinforced, like the umbrella Nicholas had forgotten in a shop miles away a week earlier that had just been returned. His two maids, who were both over five feet tall and had good eyesight, had left to become conductors on omnibuses. An elderly cook and manservant took care of the house. Anna unpacked her trunk and put her clothes way. The voyage had shown up a glaring omission in her character. She had been the only passenger whose heart had not beat faster at the thought of any particular patch of grass. There was nowhere she indelibly belonged. Yet she had climbed the stairs of this house with a classic sense of homecoming.

She opened the letters her family had sent to await her arrival, saving her father's until the end. None of the others had mentioned he had joined a regiment in the Canadian army. They hadn't known. He had wanted to give her the news before he told them. Denmark was not going to be invaded and was not at war, but he, for one, believed North Schleswig had to be won back, and the Swedes were so deplorably pro-German, the balance had to be set right. Her mother and aunts were bound to disapprove, he wrote, but he was sure Anna would not imagine the war cries around them had injected a spurt of martial blood into her father's veins. She would appreciate that friends and comrades had to be supported in a crisis. She, closest to him, would understand. Understand what? thought Anna in bewildered exasperation. That Johannes Hansen had joined a foreign army for friendship's sake and put the real issues of the twentieth century into mothballs till he finished playing soldier? There was a limit to romancing. And to absurdity. A soaring eagle had swooped down to the village pond to quack and waddle with the ducks. She wondered how the Marriots would receive the news.

"Ah!" said the friend of Nicholas's uncle, as they came

out of the study ten minutes before dinner to find a femi-
nine presence in the drawing room. "You didn't tell me we
were going to have company for dinner, my dear boy. We
shouldn't have stayed closeted for so long."

"No," said Nicholas, looking faintly puzzled to find her
there, and introducing her with her Danish credentials to
the fore. "You may be able to advise Anna about war work."

"Are you going to be with us some time, Miss Hansen?"

"Yes."

Mr. Pickford, who was a banker, waited attentive, but
that appeared to be the end of her sentence. Nicholas offered
sherry and Anna remarked she might go to a Labor Exchange
tomorrow, altering Mr. Pickford's first impression—that she
might be tongue-tied in English—to a sense that this for-
eigner was ignorant of the setup.

"They cater for the working classes and for those who
are forced to work because of a change in their circumstances," he explained. "The Central Committee on Wom-
en's Employent at Grosvenor Place would be the channel
for you. But I wouldn't recommend it. A personal introduction to a job is always the best way. I'm sure I could be of
help. So could Nicholas. There are a number of avenues.
The question is to find something suitable. And soon. I
think we may safely assume hostilities will not be pro-
longed."

At dinner he told them his wife was going to join a ladies'
committee, chaired by the Princess Victoria of Schleswig-
Holstein, to provide concerts at the front. Intent on his
soup, he watched Anna through his eyebrows and saw at a
glance he had been mistaken again, and that she might prefer a more active line of service. But was he right in thinking, not in one of the quasi-charitable or purely philanthropic
programs? No, he had thought not. Nicholas took an absent-

minded part in the conversation, saying he had heard the leading banks were having to employ women, with all the vacancies they were having to fill.

"As clerks and cashiers," said Mr. Pickford, "with much lower salaries than the men's because their standard of efficiency is much lower. But they're coming along nicely. Of course it may take a generation or more before women can look forward to being bank managers. It is one of those positions that requires a judicious blend of diplomacy, sagacity, and crystal-gazing qualities that are the result of years of experience."

Anna said she had not considered banking.

Mr. Pickford had a Canadian niece doing Voluntary Aid Detachment work, an example of how the colonies had risen magnificently to the occasion.

"She says it's quite like being back in school. The commandant reminds her of her headmistress, an the sisters who head the departments are like class mistresses. She thinks she's going to enjoy it. Twenty pounds a year and a laundry allowance," he chuckled. "It should keep young Jessica out of mischief for a while."

It made a difference to enthusiasm if you could connect the work with the cause, he said to Anna. The average factory hand couldn't. He, that is to say *she*, didn't have the degree of educated imagination to connect the piece of machinery being crafted with the trenches it was intended for. And speaking of women, the vast numbers doing men's work would raise problems after the war when men returned to their jobs, and girls like Jessica should obviously not take jobs away from women who needed them. One remedy might be to develop the dowry system, to provide women with support in time of disaster, and girls' education would probably have to include subjects that would prepare them for life, so that if misfortune did occur, they wouldn't be entirely incompetent to deal with it. Well, Anna was to let him know if he could be of assistance with an introduction.

When she left them to their port, Mr. Pickford reflected on the names of the only Danish kings he remembered apart from Canute. Harald Bluetooth and Sweyn Forkbeard. Sounded like genial ogres out of a Viking epic. One had to remember how comparatively late in the day the Scandinavians became Christianized and civilized.

Anna and Nicholas spent the next days apologizing if they brushed past each other accidentally on the stairs, or kept each other waiting for a meal. She did not think her year's absence had erected the wall between them. Where she went and what she did had always been her own affair. But by her indifference to a crisis the likes of which Europe had never known, she had betrayed her origins, not Nicholas. It had wounded him to the heart. It was why there was very little to talk about.

The Marriots welcomed her excitedly and scolded her for taking so long to get in touch with them. Mrs. Pankhurst had been granted a full release from the repeated rejailing provisions of the Cat-and-Mouse Act, and she had responded in kind by uniting the women's movement to the war effort. Anna was now so at sea in the Great Power process, and so baffled by its long reach into the most unexpected temperaments, she might have been Eastern and semibarbarous instead of merely Danish. Mr. Marriot put her into a comfortable chair and perched himself on a table with a teacup jiggling on his crossed knee. The children were on and off the rest of the furniture. The trade unions, he said, had relinquished their sacred rights for the duration. There were times when one must compromise.

Her own dear father, a militant peace-lover if ever there was one, had (with no obligation to do so) joined an army. And, added Mrs. Marriot, coming in with scones and jam, it was an opportunity to gain valuable, unheard-of experience. Did she know that women from the tenements and slums were blazing a trail? They had taken over munition works and factories. Not a crane had stopped swinging. Mrs. Marriot had placed some of the girls herself and been around some of the wooden sheds called Danger Buildings where explosives and time fuses, bombs and mines were being made. Fortunately they had more fresh air than your ordinary, hideously unhealthy factory, she said with satisfaction. They were so small you could control your own door and window.

"Dear Anna," Mrs. Marriot kissed her affectionately at the door. "Come again soon and we'll put you to work. It's wonderful to have you back. Is Mr. Wyatt well?"

Mr. Wyatt was probably quite well wherever he was. He had left for somewhere in France not long after her arrival. She was alone in the house. London, a perpetual crowd scene, made a lively contrast. People moved in droves and mobs. Omnibuses and trams were bursting with them. Before her next visit to the Marriots she had found work, and the omnibus had become her living link between days spent sleeping and nights at work. Her journeys on it filled her with the wonder of another London with its own tenacious continuity and spirit. She had a solid bond—a night shift—in common with the hard core who took the same route as herself. Like them she spent her nights on a little stool in a row of little stools with narrow gangways between them, manipulating machines that crushed, cut, and filed mountains of metal. Until she got used to it the roar was deafening. It came from the machines, the trolleys that rolled through the gangways, the network of leather belting overhead. It had not taken long to learn the three movements she had to operate. Once she had them under control, the monotony and noise combined to beat down her Himapur questions. She had no problem keeping awake at the munitions works or falling asleep at home. She could not have devised a more soothing and sedating inverse system of nights and days, one that eliminated social life and contact, and kept her working attention sharply riveted. Occasionally she had a mental picture of German women on little German stools, blonde madonnas as busy at their worktables as their British counterparts, cutting metal and piecing deadly weapons together with the same holy dedication as they had cut and stitched baby clothes. Sometimes it took on the grandeur of a vision. She was part of an international sisterhood hallowed by munitions making, the new far-reaching good works of the gentler sex. None of which need be happening if someone would ask whether all this greatness and power was really necessary.

"You didn't have to send yourself to jail like that, Anna," Mrs. Marriot protested. "Why didn't you consult me?"

But jail had its moments. Stiff and sleepy at the crack of dawn, Anna yawned and stretched and got up on a table with several of her companions one freezing morning to sing and dance the hornpipe to a tin-whistle accompaniment. It was so relaxing they did a lightning turn every now and then at the end of the shift if the supervisor was out of earshot, and weapons production took a leap forward. The German Chancellor admitted it in the Reichstag when he said England had outstripped Germany in the munitions race. So did the Tsar of all the Russias who, the factory superintendent informed them, had sent a message to his troops praising Mighty England for bearing the brunt of the war on the Allied side. Nice of 'im, 'ooever the Za might be, one of her hijinks companions whispered, adding she was ever so glad about 'is message. Anna could have worked on the land, the Marriots told her. There was plenty of work for every taste. But once you stepped into an effort for war, you had much better go to the guts of it, Anna said. You might as well make lethal weapons as plant a potato. And what with the omnibus, and going with her hornpipe companions to the trains to help them take home their walking wounded and their stretcher wounded, patriotism became the stark and unadorned fact of being tied to the same sights and sounds. The trainloads marked the end of singing and dancing, and war began in earnest.

She was sound asleep in the middle of the day with the blinds down when Nicholas came home on leave. She opened her eyes to find him sitting beside her bed. She was flooded with a passionate gratitude that he was safe and unscathed, and had been restored to her. A modern miracle had taken place this day at noon, brought Nicholas home, and ended their exile from one another. She had a feeling he was crying too, as they clung together. When she was up and dressed they lingered over a long lunch of cold leftovers, and knew they would have the rest of their lives to catch up with each other's absences in a leisurely way. Their immediate agenda was marriage, before military duty or misunderstanding separated them again.

When they came home to breakfast after their registry-office wedding Nicholas said, "You were so bowled over by your noble District Magistrate, I thought you'd never come back."

The unreality of her last days in Himapur passed over the hothouse roses of their wedding breakfast like a brief solar eclipse. An explanation was overdue, and she gave

Nicholas an account of why she had come back. Her story of one, or possibly two, unnatural deaths on a faraway hillside was as ugly as it had ever been, but lengthening casualty lists from two fronts had robbed it of its brutal impact. They were getting used to death and devastation, and it made them more merciless toward a conscious criminal act.

"Let me get this straight," said Nicholas. "Was it one murder or two?"

"I don't know, " said Anna painfully. "We can never know. And what about the spaniel?"

"Why should anyone have killed the dog?"

"I don't know," she repeated.

Under Nicholas's meticulous cross-examination it seemed she knew next to nothing, and had not taken the trouble to find out what she could have without arousing suspicion. For instance, Lulu. If Anna could have ruled out Croft by asking him one or two simple questions, it could mean Lulu might have blundered on the dog and been silenced by Henry. There were any number of angles, all of them unexplored.

"I was so stunned, I wanted to blot it all out," said Anna. "After Sir Nitin and I discussed it, I agreed with him it would be wiser to leave it alone. Under the circumstances, what could we do?"

Nicholas listed several steps she could have taken on her own. It was too late now.

"So you believe Brewster murdered his wife," he established.

Anna was taken completely unawares by the depth of her distress, and the resilient, haunting power of what Henry had done. Even Sir Nitin had not actually spelled it out in those relentless words. Anna had skirted the horror herself. She had deliberately avoided facing it, spent the next morning collecting ferns to press. There had been no other way to cope with the unthinkable.

Nicholas said with regret, "It's unlikely the law can catch up with him now, more's the pity. Still, bodies don't disappear. Murders have come to light many years after the event. But what happened to your infallible instinct, Anna? Didn't that tell you something about the man?"

Her instinct had let her down so humiliatingly, on such a vital personal matter, she would never trust it again. She felt its deep and abiding loss. She had never been so fatally mistaken about a human being, and her confidence in her own judgment was badly shaken. It made marriage a riskier undertaking than it might otherwise have been. The public certainties they had taken for granted could no longer be relied on either. Life ahead would have to consist of whatever they could salvage from public and private ruins.

"My instinct did not do very well," she admitted. "I don't know why. But you are wrong, Nicholas. I was less bowled over by Henry, as intrigued by his whole situation. And the most intriguing part of it was his obsession with Stella."

But she knew as she said it that she had fallen in love, with a vision, not merely a man. No such indivisible magic would ever come her way again. She reached for Nicholas's comforting hand across their breakfast and held it. The reluctant sun laid its pale, cool gloss on her wedding ring.

"There is the anti-imperialist side of Henry I will always admire," she confessed, and crowned him with her ultimate accolade. "He is a man ahead of his generation."

"But unfortunately a murderer," said Nicholas.

"And a murderer I never could have married. Or even loved, once I knew."

Holding the hand of his wife of an hour, Nicholas was

fairly certain she could. There was no reason why she should not up and marry a murderer if the mold-cracking mood seized her. It might one day become absolutely necessary in her own incalculable, impetuous reckonings. He and Anna were sitting here married by the skin of their teeth. It made him more thoughtful than a man usually is on his wedding day.

Anna received Henry's letter in the late autumn of 1916. It had been forwarded from Copenhagen.

Anna: though Valkyrie is how I thought of you, fresh, free, warriorlike the way you tackled the mountains and took them in your easy stride. I am addicted to them myself, and in all my years in Himapur you were the only other addict. There weren't two others like us, least of all the wretched poor who had to eke a living out of them.

If I thought I were going to come out of these trenches alive, I would be saving what I have to tell you until we met. But I've never believed I was one of a privileged few. How can I count on reprieve?

And so, about Stella, of whom you wrote to your Nicholas. I had to read your letters, and I'm only slightly sorry I did. How else would I have known you in so short a time? You managed without any cheating aids. You understood how I felt about Stella. You've dreamed of rational love yourself and you know, as few people do, that it needs more than two people. It needs the manure of a common cause. In our case there were two fierce, clashing causes, Stella's and mine, so we grew in different directions from the start. But I did not tell you the whole truth when I said our differences were political. If she had left me because she was her father's daughter, I would have accepted it and let her go without a fight. It would have been an honorable reason for parting. But her political commitment got muddled with other reasons.

I'm not certain when I lost Stella. It could have happened when Jennie was born—a difficult birth, and she was never quite as approachable afterwards—or when Khudiram was hanged, or when the Pryors came to Bihar and we met them for the first time. They had all the proverbial glitter and paraphernalia of life at the top in a state capital. A district is lonely and dull. Mine was dangerous too. The Pryors took Stella under their wing and encouraged her and Jennie to spend time with them in Lucknow and Naini Tal, and Pryor kept his word to try and get me transferred from Bihar. Unfortunately for Stella, the transfer was to Himapur. The powers that be had decreed I had to be put out to pasture in some harmless place until I got back into the proper team spirit. But the Pryors were sympathetic and asked Stella to treat their home as her own during my lengthening "convalescence." She would leave Jennie with me and go, like a child to a party. She was so happy I hadn't the heart to stop her, or to ask them not to keep sending us expensive parcels from Army-and-Navy's. Their largesse made me very uncomfortable, and their open house to Stella was making it impossible for her to settle down at home. Every parcel heralded her next departure, with a gossipy letter from Mary Pryor saying they would expect Stella to come and stay with them for the Governor's ball or the hunt or whichever event came next on the calendar, and always in plenty of time for her to prepare, pack, and travel down. In the process Lucknow became home, and Himapur a rest house on the way to it. I saw it had the day, three years ago, in the summer of 1913, when the bearer came into the garden with a package from the Pryors. We had heard the post carrier telling him it was from the Lucknow secretariat. I had barely finished taking those pictures of Stella and Jennie that hung in the dining room, when Stella jumped up and ran to take the parcel from the bearer. Her impatience would have had an excited, girlish quality but for the touch of desperation about it. I thought I saw Stella grasping a lifeline, flying toward her salvation, and I felt quite unbearably inadequate. All my objective wisdom fell apart. I followed her into the house, to our room, and she stopped me before I had begun. It was no use arguing, she said, this was the end. She was taking Jennie the next time she left and they were not coming back. There was nothing to discuss. She and Robert had discussed their plans for a life together when he was here. Until that moment, long before killing became so general, I had not known I had it in me to kill.

I knew they had been lovers for the past year. We had raked over the whole dreary business from start to finish on Pryor's visit to Himapur six weeks earlier. I thought we had worked it out, with Stella consenting to give Himapur, and me, a trial, if only for Jennie's sake. I saw what a farce his visit and our agreement had been. Stella, sitting there on her bed, holding her Army-and-Navy parcel on her lap, informed me Pryor had made the trip to tell her he had spoken to Mary about a divorce, and he would start proceedings during their home leave in the spring. Stella would have to stay put with me a little while longer, and it would be better if they did not meet or communicate for the time being, officialdom being small and nosy. By July or August the coast should be clear.

They must have thought me fair, gullible game as they made their plans during his visit. Outwardly we had talked of compromise, and we were all parties to it. All through the showdown I had insisted on solemnly, stubbornly cherishing Stella. I was the one who had talked about love. Neither of them mentioned the word. Pryor said he was "devoted" to her, they were "fond" of one another. It was all very tepid. Stella said nothing. I felt very nearly desperate, but I did not rant and rave. On the whole I was reasonable. And I felt a tremendous new tenderness for Stella, a longing to fill the gaps of my own neglect. If, for whatever reason, they had made me the prisoner at the bar, I was willing to plead guilty. I said to Pryor, since Stella wouldn't talk, "Is she pregnant? Is that the trouble? Because if she is, I'll adopt the child." They looked at each other as if I were dangerously unbalanced, and this the final travesty in my dementedness. Pryor kept a superior, detached calm. He cleared his throat and made a little speech about officers and gentlemen. And after dinner he talked about lime quarrying, wood pulp, seed potatoes, and apple orchards. He had a forest expert and commercial interests lined up. He simply couldn't understand the delay at my end. "I'm all for island paradises, Henry, but this isn't an island, you know, and it's time we put it on a footing with other hill stations, with a train connection all the way up, and other facilities." And a bandstand up on the ridge with a brass band playing Danny, You Have a Damn Fine Face, I wanted to add.

After he left, our trial period wasn't easy, nor had I expected it to be. I did believe we were keeping our bargain, and that our marriage had a chance of repair. Happiness was important to Stella, and I did all I could to make her happy. Until the day I took the picture I didn't know our open covenant had had secret clauses. There are limits to human tolerance. I had reached mine. I didn't seek a violent ending, but that is what it became. If unbalanced is how I am judged, it has helped me to understand what the law calls aberrant behavior, and given me some compassion for what men call madness. So perhaps some useful purpose has been served. Those of us who must grow old during this violent new century will need all our human resources to remain human. I know almost no one but yourself who will understand.

To put the record and your fancies straight, I don't have the makings of a Tulsidas, Anna. Except for the fact that the war has overtaken this continent like retribution, and convinces me I am sitting here for the sins of others besides my own, I do very well without the religious impulse. My sallies into mysteries beyond my intellectual grasp have all been connected with life on earth. When that became arid and pointless without Stella, the limbo I inhabited was probably the best place for me. Confessions are generally the order of the day at points of no return, but suddenly I see that I am writing to prepare you for my return. We shall see each other again, and before I come to your door I want you to forgive me for not being wholly straightforward with you when we were face to face. I feel more hopeful at the end of this letter than when I started it, that I have a life to live and I want to live it at last in accordance with my beliefs.

The letter had taken three months to reach her. The covering letter from his Commanding Officer informed her of Henry's death in the Allied offensive on the Somme. Henry, who had questioned every order on earth, had obeyed without question the order to keep advancing to his own slaughter, and had fallen in machine-gun fire during the first hour of the grimmest battle in the history of warfare.

Anna's reaction was one of icy resignation. It was too late even for sorrow. Henry—his madness in a sane cause— was beyond her judgment. How could he have expected her to understand? The travesties and grotesqueries she was expected to take in her stride! The fates would exact their dues in their inexorable ways. An entire nation, widowed or bereaved by one cataclysm, would mourn the slaughter on the Somme, but the intimate tragedy of Stella had no mourners. His letter had performed one last service. It had lifted the clouds around Stella. She had, after all, wanted to leave him for a lover, and he had prevented it. It was a story of which Anna had had higher hopes, the kind that are raised by encounters with unusual people. In the end it had been cruelly, sordidly conventional. She put the letter away to share with Nicholas when he came back. The subject was finally closed.

She waited for equilibrium to claim her during the months of Nicholas's absence, and grew tired and dismally depressed waiting for it. Madhav Rao, with his vigorous grip on the abstract, would have explained the oppressiveness of each passing day with his characteristic and confusing thoroughness. There is a general heaviness in the air when crimes are committed, Tantanna, and we are all responsible for it. No one who has lived to an adult age is innocent, Tantanna. We are guilty of each other's misdeeds, past and present, in which of course is also the future. The same wasting disease afflicts us all. And that, Anna decided, would certainly have to explain her strange and terrible heaviness of heart, for the only other explanation was that it was perfectly, calamitously possible to love a murderer, regardless of the fact that he was in his grave.

F O U R T E E N

◇

There were people whose postwar adjustments were to smaller, diminished circumstances. Anna's and Nicholas's were to visual magnificence. Nicholas bought the twelfth-century fortified manor house in Sussex, known in the county as a castle, before the war ended. It had a castle's twin-towered entrance with an oak portcullis plated and shod with iron, arched doorways, and the usual castle space and features, including, originally, a dungeon designed to shelter the garrison when the outer works fell. Before it was rebuilt it had had its own private apartments, service rooms, and a well, and everything needed to sustain life under a long siege, which was what their relationship resembled during the months following the armistice. Nicholas had his reasons for buying a castle. The idea had taken shape years earlier, before they were married, when Anna had asked him what he was going to do with a fortune. A castle was the appropriate aesthetic frame for her, and now also for abundant progeny, dynasty, ancestral property going down future ages as it had come down ages past. In a word, he wanted permanence. He had given up the diplomatic service to go into politics, a turning point directly related to diplomacy having abysmally failed to keep the balance of power. He wanted to influence policies at their source.

By 1918 Anna had acquired a medieval quiescence which should have admirably suited the setting he had chosen for her. The damage dawned on Nicholas a few days after they moved in at the end of the year, when he caught sight of her from the window of their tower bedroom. She was walking in the courtyard. Her somnambulance made the dug-up ground where some repaving had been in progress all week look like craters on the moon. She was not alone. Their son, Peter, was pulling his red Christmas engine, linked to three matching coaches, all over the flagstones. Two hysterical Labrador pups pranced and wriggled muscularly around the toy train. Sunday church bells (rung anticlockwise, Nicholas had been told), left their shining, resonant arcs high up on the frosty air. A mythic silence enveloped Anna. She was distant and deaf. She reminded him of no human being he had known. The ice-locked Baltic of rigorous Arctic winters had that aura. He thought of the mental and physical disorders, and fluctuations of mood ascribed to Scandinavian darkness. He had been away from home for most of the war and too war-racked, in any case, to register her curious condition, but she was so little given to secrecy or subterfuge, it must have been there all the time. She had stopped talking of the past or the future. She did not effervesce. She hadn't joined the jubilation at armistice, and much earlier there had been no metamorphosis with motherhood. A child was born, and Anna sighed and reverted to her interrupted dream sequences. He was not sure she had noticed the castle they were living in. If melodrama had been his style, he would have concluded she had been shot down in the machine-gun fire that had killed Henry Brewster. Nicholas's eventful relationship with Anna had been jolted by more than its fair share of surprises, but this was the first time he had had to deal with paralysis.

He actively regretted the death of Brewster. Alive, the man might have brought to justice. He would have been a human rival instead of sanctified bones interred in a French cemetery, with his farseeing, mold-breaking qualities transcending murder and marching on. Brewster was surely the theatrical extreme of Anna's effervescences. She had succumbed to a violent inner upheaval started by, almost literally, a passing stranger, a man she had known less than three months. To Nicholas's certain knowledge it had been a purely formal encounter, a supreme example of Anna's imagination in full flower. He was unable to explain its lasting havoc, but the pattern was recognizable. A morning of abstract art had made marriage unthinkable although Anna had agreed to discuss a wedding date precisely two hours earlier. A suffragette threw herself under a horse's hoofs and tore Anna's life up by the roots. Two unrelated events, except in a mind as subjective as Anna's. Isolated episodes that should have been over and done with, but weren't, much as strokes of lightning stamped erratic wires across one's vision after they had left the sky. In the course of her intensely emotional wanderings a marriage had occurred between the two of them, and the more he thought about it, the more he was inclined to put it down to a haphazard conjunction of planets that had nothing to do with a responsible, conscious decision, which, of course, was nonsense. If there were riddles that defied analysis, he hadn't come across them, and he had no regrets about the decision. There was much to be said for a step forward. It was immeasurably less artificial than a "special relationship" lived apart would have become, with joint appearances on social occasions and no Peter at the end of it, and marriage, after all, was the only relationship that guaranteed breakfast together. Nicholas was committed to steps forward, to Anna, to England, to free and ancient institutions and their continuance. He was less burdened by the ghost of Henry Brewster than by the toad under the stone that Brewster's criminal act had revealed. The two people who could have investigated the crime, however amateurishly or unsatisfactorily, had deliberately chosen to ignore it because neither of them had believed in the possibility of elementary justice. Nicholas would not otherwise have been interested in the news that Tilak was in the country, and a libel case he had brought against the English author of a book called *Indian Unrest* was to be argued in London. He asked Anna if she would like to attend the hearings.

"What's the use? They will be putting Tilak on trial for sedition again, instead of this Valentine Chirol, whoever he is, for whatever he has written."

She had read in the *Daily Herald*, edited obviously by the ghost of Brewster, that the Government of India had identified itself with this Chirol and was backing him to the hilt with its own anti-Tilak reports. If the government was on his side, Chirol had to win. In her opinion the judge, like the ones who had tried Tilak for sedition, would be vitriolically anti-Tilak. She saw no point in attending prejudiced hearings. Her convictions at any rate were staunchly in place. Too staunchly, it struck Nicholas. Anna had been humane, not political. This was Brewster's mantle. But whoever's, the stumbling block was the toad. Justice converted into a Byzantine farce, if what she said was true. Nicholas had a foretaste of global repercussions if the public, apart from Anna and the unvanquishable corpse of Brewster, saw it that way. He found himself sitting through Sir John Simon's seven-hour argument as he opened the case for Tilak in January, and was present again at its conclusion in February when the jury came in with a unanimous verdict in favor of Chirol.

"What did you expect of a prejudiced judge who is a liar?"

Anna commented in a spirited return to daylight from her winter equinox.

Nicholas was profoundly disturbed. It could be Anna's unorthodox juxtapositioning of words that could never, in standard usage, sit side by side in an English sentence. But she repeated her charge that the prejudiced judge had told a cool pack of lies. Tilak had never wanted to sabotage the war effort by asking Indians not to join the army. Quite the reverse. He'd been doing his best to push them into it. True, he had been definite about not remaining in the empire; nor would the judge and jury have wanted to, as servants and load carriers. Common sense, not treason. Nowhere in Nicholas's empire would Tilak get a just hearing, which was one of her exaggerations. For what it was worth, Tilak was getting on like a house on fire with the Labour movement. It had offered him a platform, and he and his colleagues were addressing workers' meetings from Glasgow to Southampton. Ramsay Macdonald had pledged the Independent Labour party's support to the Indian struggle for independence and introduced Tilak at a political meeting as "the very embodiment of the spirit of resistance which is manifest in India today." Anna read the quote from the *Daily Herald,* and Brewster couldn't have put it better himself. The redoubtable Tilak, trailed by Scotland Yard, and threatened with financial ruin by the loss of his case, had presented a two-thousand-pound check to the Labour Party. He was glad to inform them a fund had been started for him in India. M. K. Gandhi had presided over the public meeting in Bombay to launch it, and the money was pouring in. Nicholas, not ready to disband his empire, retired to his study to consider the decline of British justice. Bickering little identities had become sovereign nations, monarchies had fallen, three empires had been wiped off the map, because justice had not been done.

He drove back from London one June evening with the news that he had been introduced to Robert Pryor at his club.

"The rumor is he's going to be appointed Governor of Bombay Presidency. I've asked him and his wife to lunch on Sunday. I thought you'd like to meet them."

There was nothing Anna wanted less, and he sensed her overpowering reluctance to meet the Pryors. The subject of Himapur was closed. Sir Nitin's Christmas card from Allahabad every year was her only connection with that bit of her past, and Sir Nitin had the tact never to refer to it. Nicholas, unpenitent, said he would take the Pryors for a stroll through the grounds and show them the Norman windows in the church. Anna could join them whenever she was ready.

At noon a car door shut, voices met, there was a flurry in the courtyard below, ending in Peter talking industriously to himself as he dragged his wooden cart carrying clothes-peg passengers along the flagstones. She heard Peter's mutter as the cart was picked up and set down on the grass beyond the new paving. Nothing more. The soft rain accompaniment to her silences started and stopped when she saw the sun was shining. Summer was at its tranquilizing height. Memory caught up with the time, the place, the room. Anna recalled her geographical location and role, and went down a winding turret staircase, out through a slit side entrance, stopping to speak to Peter's passengers on her way across the green to the church where her guests would now be.

The day was so radiantly bright she had to acccustom her eyes to its twilit interior. In semidarkness opposite, a resurrected Christ rose from his tomb, cross in hand. Two Roman soldiers slept soundly in the next wall panel. Christ appeared to a single apostle in the third. Sunrays lit the stained glass at the south end with a luminous fire. The jeweled blue and ruby of the painter's art glanced off a copper engraved plate listing the vicars since 1405. And Anna saw Pryor, neat and convex in a halo of light, having an animated chat with Nicholas. She stood quite still, a hand involuntarily raised to her cheek, as though the ineffable mystery of why one loved or stopped loving, had the grazing edge of a butterfly's wing. They walked to the village, Pryor between her and Nicholas, stepping buoyantly on the balls of his feet, rhapsodic about the church and the countryside. His wife had not come on a tour because of a twisted ankle. She waited for them at the castle, propped by cushions on the sofa against the castle's unique five-lancet window, with her foot resting on a stool. Pryor introduced her with a delight and astonishment, "My wife Stella."

Skirts had ascended, waists descended. Figures had flattened and everyone's billowing hair had been shingled. A *chaddar* covering a woman from top to toe could not have provided a completer disguise. But this beyond doubt was Stella. Nicholas's supporting arm around Anna's shoulders helped her forward. She greeted Pryor's wife and excused herself to see about lunch. When she came back they were pleasurably settled for life. Sunshine repatterned the carpet. Nicholas had dispensed gin and lime and was enquiring what postwar changes there were going to be in India in the way of administrative reforms, so important if they were going to keep the loyalty of the middle classes.

"No reason why there should be any changes," said Pryor. "We've got our hands full."

"With?" asked Anna.

"Well, chiefly the mood. It's changed. They don't see us as morally superior any more. The war did that, Europeans falling out among themselves. The old imperial magic is gone. Things aren't what they used to be when a man we could trust implicitly, Sir Nitin Basu, gives up his knighthood as a protest against the trouble in Amritsar."

"That's why your experience is needed, darling," said his Stella.

He was sitting beside her on the sofa, bathed in the same streaming golden incandescence.

"It won't be easy," he said. "There's been a dramatic change of mood. The Indian army has had fighting experience all over the world. Indian troops helped us to take Jerusalem and Baghdad in '17. A fine lot of officers and men."

He reviewed the grave consequences for imperial rule of fine native soldiering, and access to arms and rank.

"In other words, the time is ripe for a crucial step forward," Nicholas persisted.

"On the contrary. Shelburne prophesied the day we recognized American independence, Great Britain would be reduced to a miserable little island, and from there would sink into total insignificance and become a Denmark or a Sardinia. He was wrong. But we're faced with the prospect now if we ignore the signs."

"Anna is Danish," said Nicholas.

"Are you, Mrs. Wyatt? I thought you were Swedish."

"Anna thinks every country should sink into total insignificance as fast as possible."

The Pryors warmly appreciated the joke.

They were all at their most convivial over lunch. Nicholas patiently pursued cautious reform, while he secretly celebrated his discovery of the body. He had been right. Bodies did not disappear. Brewster could proceed to sainthood and eternal rest. He mentioned Anna's eleven months in India, three of them in a hill station. Pryor, giving his food the attention it deserved, said between mouthfuls that hill stations did not have to be the profitless places they were. Their resources hadn't begun to be tapped. Where Stella's first husband had been was an example.

"Did you come across a sadistic man called Croft who bullied his wife?" asked Stella. "She was terrified of him. I'm sorry I wasn't nicer to her."

"She's dead," said Anna.

"He probably pushed her over the hill," said Stella serenely, "just the sort of thing he'd do. I don't know how they ever got together. Poor Henry's dead too. His death made up for everything, didn't it, darling?"

"A capable man, one of our best," was Pryor's epitaph, "but he never did understand the ideology of rule."

He looked down at his plate, crestfallen to find it empty. The casserole dish was scraped clean too, except for a sprig of parsley, but he cheered up when the raspberries arrived, and outlined the measures the government must take to keep Indian nationalism in check.

Anna deserted small talk with Stella to say she had been at a political meeting while she was there, a dazzling affair, and she was sure it couldn't be kept in check.

"How could you possibly know what they were saying when you didn't speak the language?" asked Stella, mildly interested.

They were charmed by her reply. Pryor said come, come, she was being far to modest. All the Swedes he knew spoke excellent English. She could have been no exception, judging by her fluency now, and he understood she was fluent in French too.

In the afternoon another walk around the village for the men left Anna with Stella Pryor. Nicholas had not twisted her ankle but he had masterfully planned the day around the twist. Drinking coffee in the garden Stella was a sweetly blurred version of Madhav Rao's portrait, but she had her own clear-cut angle of vision unobstructed by other people's points of view. Government House in Bombay had a glorious beach, but dark heavy furniture. The challenge for Robert. Life with Robert. He doted on Jennie. The first thing he had done for Jennie was buy her a dog.

"He went to enormous trouble to get her a spaniel exactly like ours."

"What happened to yours?"

"She died the day before we left, bitten by a scorpion. It must have got into the dry grass the bearer used to line Juliet's basket with. Jennie cried so much I thought she'd never get over it. But we gave Juliet a nice little burial ceremony above the picnic spot we used to go to, and that consoled her. Henry said Juliet would probably be preserved. There's a lot of lime in the soil there."

Anna and Nicholas saw their guests off after tea. The car started, the Pryors waved and moved past them, taking the long light summer evening away with them. Anna heard Nicholas say it had been quite a day. He talked quietly as they walked back to the castle arm-in-arm. He was pleased the Pryors had stayed so long. It had given him an opportunity to acquaint himself with the official mind, and obviously something drastic had to be done about its shortsightedness. But above all, how he and Anna had misjudged Brewster, and what a relief it all was! No evil to contend with there. Anna's instinct had not let her down and now she'd be able to put the whole thing in its proper perspective. In his own experience, facts were facts. Things as a rule were what they appeared to be. Fat people were fat because they ate too much and not because they resented their younger brothers. Those who sat around never uttering weren't darkly, sinisterly brooding. They were waiting till they had something to say. He went into his study to draft a note about the urgency of gradual colonial reform.

Anna entered an unfamiliar turret bedroom. People wake up with a shock in palaces and huts, Tantanna, in the middle of a jungle or on a cliff's edge, not knowing how or why they are there, or who they are. Every day these cases are reported in the newspaper, tza, how do you not know? It is simple confusion, Madhav Rao had said, when this lifetime gets temporarily displaced by events of the lifetime before. With his penchant for leaving his listener suspended in the cosmos, he had not explained how the lost and wandering regained themselves. Anna lay down, letting a soft weightless haze of fatigue slip over her. She was back at dinner with Henry, Stella fleeing on the wall behind her. She spoke frankly to Henry about her fears, and could hardly believe she had no reason to leave. The candles and silver shone with a rare prophetic brilliance. There was nothing between them and their future. Anna lay wondering what had made her think their common future hung on the strand of his guiltlessness.

"It doesn't matter whether Henry was guilty of a crime or not," she said, faintly puzzled, to Nicholas when he came in.

"I suppose not, now that he's dead."

But Anna meant the Stella factor, even sturdier in her absence than her presence, and the grossly unequal distribution of love.

The footnote about Gayatri's grandmother in Jason's paper on Tilak's leadership of the Congress was two pages long.

He wanted to drive out and discuss it with Anna but they kept postponing a visit to her. Gayatri positively dreaded it; so afraid her next visit to her grandmother would be her last, she preferred not to go. They were still asleep when the telephone rang. Jason answered it. Age and fragility had not affected Anna's optimism or her voice.

"My dear boy. I have woken you too early."

Gayatri took the receiver from him, alert and tearful. "We're wide awake now, Gran. It's lovely to hear your voice."

"Pack up then and come along for the weekend," urged Anna. "The castle needs occupiers. When your grandfather bought it we didn't know we'd have only one child and the child would have only one child, and India would be their home."

Guests of assorted nationalities had occupied its bedrooms most weekends and come to meals on other appointed days before Nicholas died, and Anna had her own circle of faithfuls. The castle was not as bleak as she made it sound. Gayatri had spent her holidays in it. During those years the castle was in Delhi, the Lodi tombs and the Qutab Minar in Sussex, and Sussex in Denmark, a muddle Anna had approved, saying we were all each other's history. For all her gifts, or because of them, Anna still didn't see the impenetrable barriers, the utter impossibility of this comfortable Western world being part of that other's anxiety and pain. Anna and her mother were both changers, but of oh such different worlds.

"What's there to cry about?" Jason soothed, "She sounded wonderful."

"I know."

But Gayatri wept with a purpose as she dressed, preparing herself for the ordeal of Anna's death. Rehearsals would put her flawlessly in control of her emotions when the time came. She went into the kitchen where cooking breakfast lulled her.

This time arrival at the castle was hard to bear. It would be sold after Anna. Gayatri's placid Western world, the knowledge that one day in it passed like another—so unlike never knowing what tomorrow would bring in India—had been more palpable at the castle than anywhere else. It was absent today. She was frantically close to tears again with her warm, brown cheek pressed against her grandmother's transparent face, but Anna was her irrepressible self. She took them off to see her present to them, the cottage soon to be theirs. When they came back, the footnote on Hima-pur revived anecdotes she had almost forgotten. It was a problem, she confessed, to visualize the place, the people, the tumult of feelings she had felt. Himapur was becoming the primal world one left behind in childhood, the lost realm of infinite detail one repossessed only in dreams.

"We forget those as soon as we wake. For that matter, we can never be sure of anything we remember. There's no absolute certainty about any evidence."

Jason disagreed. There was historical evidence.

"Who knows where any of it will be a hundred years hence?" smiled Anna. "I don't care whether King Arthur lived, or didn't, as long as we have the Holy Grail."

When she retired to her room to rest after lunch Jason and Gayatri took a rug and pillows into the garden.

"Where is Himapur?" asked Jason, lying face down, the sun on his back.

"Do you mean longitude and latitude?"

"I mean, is there such a place?"

"There must be."

"And were the people real, apart from Tilak?"

"They must have been. Gran always said she met a kindred soul in Henry Brewster."

"Kindred spirits are hard to find. We sometimes have to invent them out of sheer need," murmured Jason worriedly into his pillow.

"She says she invented me. She was so disappointed the world hadn't changed enough in her lifetime, she had to hurry it along. Jason, are you listening? My father was not the sort to branch out and marry a dynamo on the other side of the world all on his own. Jason?"

Gayatri got up, took in the floweriness of the garden and each of its trees with her own and the eye of restless memory, and steeled herself to take formal leave of her castle spaces and corners. The flagstones of the courtyard disappeared one by one under her departing footsteps. She went through the downstairs rooms where Anna had told her, or somehow made her aware, of her imaginary voyages back over the water to India. The sea had had the languor of a lake, the light a perfect purity, and Anna had been journeying to revise an evening of her past. Pencil in hand, one could do that so easily on a page, insert a question where it belonged. It was Nicholas who had arranged the first of their actual voyages back, on his missions of gradual reform. After his empire, too, had gone the way of every other, they had sat side by side at Peter's marriage ceremony in Delhi. The bride's political activism lay dormat under her red and gold bridal finery, but when they had first met her, Anna's startled comment to Nicholas had been, "Me, when I was young!" And she never had got over that wonder of a torch passed amazingly, unexpectedly on. The world would remain more or less as it was. Greatness and power would never be put away as angels dancing on a pin had been. The living would keep saying, we had the power to fulfill our dreams but for complex reasons which you, my dear, would never understand, we couldn't fulfill them. It is regrettable, but human sacrifice could not be, can never be, avoided. But in this very world Peter was marrying this flame of a girl. And then, not any child, but Gayatri, was born. The fact was, Anna had assured Gayatri since infancy, that there were mysteries. Why and whom one loved was the most ineffable of them. And one loved certain people so dearly, so without beginning or end, that their birth or death made no difference to the loving.

Gayatri went up to her grandmother's room by their favorite side entrance, conscious of her every farewell footfall on the winding stair. The room was naturally cool, winter and summer. As a child she had often mistaken day for night in it. One hardly noticed the modern furniture or electric bulbs in niches hewn out of stone for candles. The old silk scroll from a Buddhist monastery held together by its rose and royal blue embroidery, had been glassed-in for protection. Its narrow wood base no longer tapped the wall in a breeze as it had through Gayatri's childhood. Everything rested, Anna stillest of all on her big canopied bed, looking like a person to whom things happened, and not the enchantress and mold cracker of family legend. She gave a flickering sigh and Gayatri held her breath. A hairline separated sleep from waking, or not-waking, at Anna's age. She stood tense and agonized at the foot of the bed, uncertain which it would be.

In a little while she heard the lawn mower churning fresh grass, a bird, tiny and distant, chirping through it, followed by other time-erasing summer sounds, and breathed again. She eased herself gently to the floor and closed her eyes in an effort to summon all she knew of Anna, in all the ways one remembers. Talk overheard and stories told dissolved into what she had always known deep down. She saw a miniature Anna's serious face under a fur hat, skates over her shoulder. Older Annas whose religion had been sun, snow, water, in acts and postures of worship. Anna and Nicholas in a newspaper picture the day he won his election to Parliament, another later when she won hers and they became the only couple to sit on opposite sides of the House, living their triumphant parallel lives. The good, satisfying memories that folded peacefully away, Anna had called them. The ones that kept one alive and stirring belonged to lost opportunity, the road one might have taken, for there was no release from the embrace of things that had never happened. Imagine, Anna laughed, the horror of getting everything we want, and what lumps and clods we'd be but for our yearnings. Oddly enough, we are the legacy of our aches, of plans that never came to pass. Gayatri saw it, the limitless sky, rocks, a track leading up to frozen mountain passes, a spring below, and a man and woman drying their hair with the rapture of pilgrims transformed by a dip in the Ganges. The woman picked up her blouse and gasped as the pearl brooch on it slipped out, fell off the ledge into the roaring water, glittered, and was gone like all material things. They laughed victoriously and turned to each other, the only two on earth, stripped of their belongings and delirious with the joy of it.

Anna's turret room blazed with long-remembered joy.

"Are you there, my own?" Anna's incredibly young voice sighed half in her sleep.

Whether it was meant for someone real or imaginary, Gayatri responded, quick and loving, "Here I am."

She went downstairs, hungry and thirsty, to put the kettle on for tea. The fact is, she reminded herself, we can't even hope for things we can't imagine, one world out of many, love everlasting, and all the rest.

G L O S S A R Y

ayah—nurse, nanny

bearer—manservant

Bhagavad Gita—scripture, part of the Mahabharata

biri—hand-rolled local cigarette

Brahma—one of the three supreme gods of Hinduism, the other two being Vishnu and Shiva

Brahmo Samaj—Society of God, a movement to reform Hinduism, founded in Calcutta in 1828

chaddar—enveloping sheet

Company Bahadur—literally, Valiant Company, referring to the East India Company

dal—lentils

jaggery—coarse brown sugar made from the jaggery palm

kheer—milk pudding

khud—ravine

Murdabad—Death to (part of a slogan)

PWD—Public Works Department

syce—groom

tantric—occult

tiffin—lunch

Vande Mataram—Hail Motherland

Zindabad—Long live (part of a slogan)